Book Two

Sea Dragons
From the World Below

THE BLUE PEARL
SERIES

Mark & Nadia

DISCLAIMER

This book is a work of fiction. Names, characters, businesses, places, events, locales, and incidents are either the products of the author's imagination or used in a fictitious manner. Any resemblance to actual persons, living or dead, or actual events is purely coincidental.

ISBN 979-8-218-31847-5 (Paperback)

Angelfish Publications
United States of America

Cover Design © 2023 created by our talented friend Mr. Ian Ouellette.
All rights reserved. Used with permission.

Original Artwork for The Blue Pearl Series © 2023 created by the legendary artist Mr. Bill Golliher.
All rights reserved. Used with permission.

Printed in the United States of America.

DEDICATION

This book is dedicated to our beloved parents: Shirley & Ernie Schaper (Mark's parents), and Pop & Joost Kaligis (Nadia's parents).

Mark's Dedication

I previously mentioned in our first book about having had a wonderful mom, but I also wanted to share a few things about my great dad.

My dad was a baseball coach and a darn good one! He was well respected in the community, and he was very proud of the difference that he made in the lives of so many young boys who played for him over the years.

As a player on his team, I learned the values of teamwork, respect for your opponent, and of always trying your best, regardless of whether you won or lost. Important "lessons" that have stayed with me throughout my life.

He is never far from my heart, and I thank God for having him in my life. Miss you, Dad! Love, Mark.

Nadia's Dedication

In the second book of the Blue Pearl Series, we share a story about family, friendship, love, and forgiveness. These are the same values that were taught by my beloved parents to me and my three other siblings.

Being a pastor's daughter, I learned that mom and dad loved us unconditionally and I witnessed the incredible power of forgiving others. My parents practiced what they preached in their daily lives, and it set a great example for all of us to follow.

They have been gone now for a few years and I miss them so very much, but I will always carry them close in my heart.

Love you forever, Mom and Dad! Your daughter, Nadia.

~ A Graduation Surprise ~

"MOVE!!" Mark Tanner's inner-voice screamed at the clock mounted on his classroom's wall. But the clock simply refused to move! He wondered if maybe some sneaky someone had glued the clock's hands in one place to permanently keep it from moving. In an age of seemingly never-ending conspiracy theories, his sounded just as plausible as any of the other ones he had heard recently. He could almost hear the voice of Rod Serling saying, *"Imagine if you will, a room where time itself ceases to exist, where there is NO possibility of any kind of escape!"* Mark involuntarily shuddered at the thought that such a place could actually exist somewhere out there in the vastness of the universe.

Finally, mercifully, the bell did ring. Mark gathered his books and quickly made his way towards the door and his impending freedom. He quickly disappeared into the vast sea of humanity that had suddenly now filled the hallways to over-flowing. Like a pink salmon swimming upstream, he cleverly navigated his way ever forward. As he exited the building and felt the warm rays of the sun upon his face, he smiled, knowing that he had successfully triumphed once again! A sharp, shrill blast from a very familiar car horn sounded from somewhere close by, and Mark immediately turned in the direction of the sound. His older brother Michael's red Chevelle would be his "ticket to ride" on this brilliant summer day.

Michael was home for the summer after completing his first year of studies at the University of Auburn. He was studying marine biology and he had taken to it like the proverbial "fish to water." Mark would smile whenever Michael began talking about how one day, he was going to be exploring the undersea world. Mark had already discovered for himself how amazing it truly was. He wanted to tell his brother and his mom of the great adventure he had experienced beneath the ocean's waves, and how he and Sasper had helped save both the

5

undersea and the surface worlds from the evil wizard Ka-Lan, but he had promised to keep Mindar a secret and he would NOT break that promise even for his own family.

Mark and the Royal Princess of Mindar had kept in touch by using the aquarium in his bedroom as their communication device, but Madison had put the complete kibosh on any actual in-person visits. She was concerned that it might put Mindar at risk of being discovered by the surface world. Mark understood the why, but he sure didn't like it. But what could he do? This is how the situation was, and it didn't show any signs of changing anytime soon. All he could do was hope that somehow, in some yet unrevealed way, everything would work out in the end. *Hope* is a very small 4-letter word in the English dictionary, but it can also be one of the most powerful forces in the universe.

As Michael's 1970 Chevelle cruised down the highway headed for home, Mark's mind drifted away to thoughts of Mindar and of Nadee, the beautiful princess who lived there. What was she doing right now? Was she thinking about him, too? He hoped that she was. Was this what it felt like to be in love with someone? If not, it sure did feel like it.

"Earth to Mark! Come in, please!" The sound of Michael's voice abruptly intruded into Mark's wistful thoughts.

"Huh? What?" Mark stammered as he returned to reality.

"Dude! I really wish you'd stop doing that!! It's like you're here one minute and then you're completely gone the next! I don't know where you go all the time but it's sure got a hold on you, bro'! I know I nicknamed you *dreamer* but over this past year you've really taken this thing to the next level!"

"SORRY!" Mark muttered.

Mark suddenly felt a strong urge inside of him to tell his older brother EVERYTHING! About Mindar, about Nadee, but he just as quickly decided against it. His startling and completely unexpected revelation might have caused Michael to lose control of the Chevelle and smash head-long into one of the many trees that lined the highway.

At the age of ten, Mark had discovered comic books. The thrilling adventures that he read in those pages had granted him access to another world. Now, he was experiencing first-hand some of the challenges that came with being an actual super-hero. Such as, keeping secrets from the people that were closest to you. One of the Tanner family house rules was to always tell the truth. Telling lies would just create even bigger problems for everyone involved, because sooner or later, the truth would come out. It was better to just deal with the situation as it was and then find a way to move past it.

His dad had been raised on a small farm in Iowa and he remembered him saying, *"If you plant a watermelon seed in the ground, a watermelon will grow, I promise you."* But now, here he was, keeping important things from his family, and it was really starting to weigh on him. He knew that at some point he would have to tell them the whole truth from beginning to end. But that moment would just have to wait a while longer.

As Michael pulled his car into the family driveway Mark immediately began to think about his next talk with Nadee, which was supposed to happen later that night. The Tanner boys quickly scampered up the steps of their 2-story home and were greeted at the door by the wonderfully enticing smell of KFC. They looked at each other and grinned!

"Mom? We're home!" Michael called out. Samantha Tanner looked up from the kitchen table where she was seated and smiled. Her two young boys had somehow, and seemingly overnight, grown into two fine young men. She motioned for them to wash their hands and get themselves seated at the kitchen table.

"I thought I'd surprise you tonight. I know how much you both love KFC," she said.

"Way to go, Mom!" Mark said happily as he reached for a piece of delicious fried chicken.

"You definitely get my vote for *Mom of the Year*," Michael added.

"So, tell me about your day. Anything exciting happen?" she asked.

Mark was about to answer her when his mom's cellphone phone rang.

"Don't answer it, Mom! Just let it go to voicemail," Michael advised her.

Samantha Tanner glanced down at the caller ID, and she immediately recognized the number.

"CAN'T! It's my District Manager. He said he was going to call me tonight about something important, so I better take this call."

"Hello? Mr. Wilson...Good evening, Sir," she began.

The happy look on their mother's face quickly faded as she listened to the voice on the other end.

"But, Sir, my son's high school graduation ceremony is this Friday."

What followed next was a rapid-fire set of responses.

"Yes, Sir. No, Sir. I understand, Sir. I'll make sure it gets done, Sir."

Finally, there was a firm response of "Goodnight, Mr. Wilson."

Samantha just stood there holding the cellphone in her right hand and staring straight ahead blankly.

"Mom?" Michael asked with concern in his voice.

"I have to fly to Philly tomorrow morning, and I won't be back until late Sunday night," she said softly.

"But Mom, that means you'll miss my graduation ceremony!!" Mark said with anguish in his voice.

"I am so sorry! But I must do this," she said.

Mark jumped up from the kitchen table and quickly headed up the stairs to his room.

"Let me talk to him, Mom," and Michael got up from the kitchen table and followed after him.

Samantha put her face into her hands, and she began to cry.

As Michael stood in the doorway to Mark's room, he could see his younger brother just sitting on the bed and staring straight ahead at his aquarium.

Michael slowly entered the room and sat down along side of him.

"This really sucks big-time, bro'!" Michael said shaking his head.

"It's my high school graduation ceremony and now BOTH of my parents aren't even going to be there!" Mark said angrily.

"Hey! You've still got me, bro'. I'll be there cheering for you!" and he tried to offer his younger brother an encouraging smile.

Suddenly, they heard the voice of their mom calling for them to come back downstairs.

As they re-entered the family kitchen Samantha looked directly at Mark.

"I just made a phone call. He should be here in just a few minutes."

"Who'd you call, Mom?" Mark asked curiously.

"You'll see," she replied.

There was the sound of a car pulling into their driveway followed by a quick toot on the horn.

"That must be him now," Samantha said, and she smiled.

As they exited out the front door, Michael and Mark's eyes widened. They just stood there staring at what was now sitting very proudly in their driveway.

A classic 1965 royal blue Mustang convertible!

Mr. Harris, a long-time neighbor, who had been great friends with their dad, got out of the car. He handed the keys to Samantha, smiled, and then turned to begin his walk back home.

"Enjoy your car, Mark. She's a real beauty!" he called out as he was leaving.

Mark stood there completely stunned.

"Thanks, Ed. I really appreciate your help with this," Samantha called out to him.

Mark's mom then turned to him and said, "Your father gave me some very strict instructions. You were supposed to get this right after the graduation ceremony, but since everything's

10

changed now, I think he'd be alright with you getting it tonight," and she held out the keys to Mark.

"A '65 convertible Mustang?? Am I dreaming this??" Mark exclaimed.

"I love my Chevelle, but man...little brother you just hit the JACKPOT!!" Michael shouted.

Mark put his arms around his mom and squeezed her tight. "THANKS Mom! I LOVE the car!"

"Well, don't just stand there you two...go check 'er out!" she said excitedly.

Samantha smiled as her two boys raced for the Mustang and quickly climbed inside. They just sat there appreciating this special moment.

"Total game-changer, bro'!" Michael said to his younger brother.

"What do you mean...game-changer?" Mark asked him.

"A really hot car equals really hot girls, bro'!" and Michael grinned.

Mark smiled, and he whispered, "Thanks, Dad."

About a half-hour later Mark and Michael finally came back inside the house.

Samantha looked up from reading her newest book, "The Blue Pearl Series" by Mark & Nadia. Sasper had been keeping her company, but now he had fallen fast asleep and was curled up by her feet.

"Alright, I guess that's enough excitement for one night. Time for you two to get some sleep," Samantha said.

"C'mon, lil' brother," and Michael slapped Mark on the back.

After saying goodnight to Michael, Mark plunked himself down on his bed and waited for Nadee's call. A few seconds later his 36-gallon aquarium was enveloped once more in blue energy, and an image began to appear in it.

"Hey!" Mark said.

"What is this look, Mark? I cannot tell if you are happy or sad," she said with some concern.

"A little bit of both, actually," Mark answered her.

"Both? I do not understand," Nadee questioned.

"Well, I'm happy because my dad just gifted me this really cool car for a graduation present," Mark shared.

"That is WONDERFUL! Then, why are you so sad?" she asked.

"I found out tonight that my mom won't be at my graduation ceremony," Mark said softly.

"Oh, I am so sorry, Mark. I know how much you wanted her to be there."

"It's NOT her fault! Her boss is making her fly to Philly tomorrow, and she won't get back until sometime Sunday night," Mark explained.

"I know she would be there if it were possible," Nadee offered.

"I know...it's just that..." and his voice trailed off.

"I understand. This is supposed to be a special family moment for all of you."

"Listen, I'm really sorry, but I'm not in much of a talking-mood tonight. Is it okay if we just make this a short call?" Mark asked her.

"Of course, Mark. I understand completely. We can talk again some other time," she suggested.

Suddenly, there was a soft knock on the door to Mark's bedroom.

"Sweetheart? Are you still awake?" his mom asked.

"Gotta' go! Talk soon! Bye!" Mark whispered to Nadee.

Mark got up from his bed and headed over towards the door. He took one last look back at his aquarium before opening the door to his room.

"Hey! Just thought I'd check on you one more time," his mom said, and she smiled at him.

Mark sat down on his bed and his mom sat down along side of him.

"I feel absolutely terrible!" she said looking into his eyes.

"It's NOT your fault, Mom. Things just happen... sometimes," Mark said to her reassuringly.

"Does getting your new car tonight help you to feel a little bit better?" she asked hopefully.

"Are you kidding me!?! That car is beyond... AMAZING!" Mark said with a big smile.

"Your father was so excited the day that he bought it for you. I'm sure he's smiling somewhere right now knowing how happy this makes you."

"I'm sure he is, too, mom," Mark agreed.

13

"Well, it's getting pretty late. I just wanted to make sure you were really okay," she said to him.

"Thanks, Mom! I'm okay. Really."

Samantha then got up to leave but not before giving her youngest son one big final hug. As she looked over his shoulder suddenly her eyes widened.

"Something wrong?" Mark asked her nervously.

"It's your room...it looks a little extra blue-y tonight. I just happened to notice it."

"It's probably just some trick of the moonlight, Mom." Mark quickly responded.

"Ooooo-k! But your drapes are pulled completely SHUT! There is NO light of any kind getting into your room from anywhere that I can see," and she began to look around the room.

"Listen, I'm pretty tired and tomorrow's gonna' be a really big day for me so I need to..."

"Get some sleep? Okay! We'll just say our goodnights then and I'll see you in the morning."

"I love you, Mom!" Mark said to her.

"I love you, too," and she closed the door to his room softly behind her as she left.

Mark lay back on his bed and let out a huge sigh of relief. His secret was still SAFE!

A few minutes later there was another soft knock on the door.

"Looks like we forgot about someone," Samantha said to Mark.

"Who?" Mark asked.

The door opened slightly and a very wobbly Sasper entered the room and immediately crawled under the bed.

"Sleep well, you two," Samantha said, and she gently closed the door for a final time.

~ An Unexpected Visitor at School ~

As sunlight greeted them the next day, Mark and Michael wolfed down their breakfast and then raced out the door hoping that what had happened the night before wasn't just a dream.

They smiled! The classic '65 Mustang was still sitting there in the driveway.

"Listen, I know you're super-excited and I'd be, too, but just be smart out there today, okay? Pay attention to the road and don't take any chances," Michael advised his younger brother.

"I'll be extra careful, I promise!" Mark said.

Mark sat down in the Mustang, turned the ignition key, and the car immediately roared to life.

Samantha and Michael watched as Mark carefully backed the car out of the driveway.

"He's a good driver, Mom. You don't have to worry about him," Michael said to her.

"Worrying is what we moms do. It comes with the job," she replied.

Mark waved goodbye to them and then he quickly headed down Maple Street.

Mark felt...ECSTATIC! Here he was cruising down the road in a classic Mustang!

As he slowly pulled into the school parking lot, he could feel the eyes of his fellow classmates looking at him...or rather, to be more precise, at his new car!

He found a place to park, put the roof up, turned the ignition key off, and climbed out of the car.

From out of nowhere, Sandy Williams suddenly appeared, and she stood directly in front of him.

The very same Sandy Williams he'd had a huge crush on ever since the 8th grade! ...And who, to this moment in time, had said a total of about ten words to him.

She smiled invitingly at him, then focused her full attention on the Mustang behind Mark.

"Nice car, Mark. Maybe we could go for a ride sometime?" and she winked at him.

"Sorry, Sandy. I'm, eh, running late for class," and he quickly walked away from her.

"What just happened!?!" he thought to himself. *"Did I really just totally blow-off Sandy Williams!?!"*

Michael was RIGHT! Everything had now suddenly changed for him. There was a noticeable extra bounce in his step as he made his way that morning down the familiar hallways of Platt high school.

The day itself passed rather quickly, until only his algebra class remained.

But as he entered the room it wasn't the always smiling and somewhat chubby face of Mr. Patrick Fischer that greeted him today. NO! NOT even close!

A strikingly beautiful, dark-haired young woman was sitting behind the desk! Their eyes met for just a moment, and she smiled at him, and it did *something* to him.

He made his way over to his seat and glanced down at the surface of his desk. When he looked up, the beautiful young woman was looking right back at him.

As the last student finally meandered into the room and got seated, the young woman stood up and moved to the front of the desk.

"Good afternoon, everyone!" she began.

"As all of you can plainly see, I am NOT Mr. Fischer. I will be subbing for him today. My name is...Miss Shanti."

"I'm sure you're all anxious to get out of here and enjoy this beautiful day, so I'm going to give you an opportunity to do just that."

She began to slowly walk around the room, passing out a piece of paper to each student as she went along. When she had given out the very last one, she turned and addressed the entire class.

"On the paper that I've placed in front of you is a word problem. The moment you come up with the correct answer to it, you are free to leave."

A wave of excitement quickly swept over the entire classroom. However, NOT everyone in the room felt that way. Mark glared down at the white paper sitting there on his desk. *"WORD PROBLEMS! Why did it have to be a word problem?!?"*

Superman had kryptonite, Indiana Jones had snakes, and Mark had word problems! His mind was simply NOT wired that way and they were as unsolvable to him as a Rubik's cube puzzle!

"You may begin," Miss Shanti announced to the class.

Over the next 45 minutes Mark watched in pure frustration as one by one his fellow classmates succeeded in solving the word problem and happily exited the classroom.

Now, he and Dorothy Ozoda were the only ones left in the room. Out of the corner of his eye he saw her smile, and then she raced to the front of the room.

Every single one of his classmates had succeeded in solving the word problem and earned their precious freedom. He fought the urge to grab the piece of white paper and crumble it into a tiny ball! He glanced up at the clock and took some consolation in knowing that in just 10 more minutes he, too, would finally be able to leave.

He decided to have a little fun in the time left to him by creating his own word problem. He picked up his pen and started to write on the white paper. *How many puffers would it take to remove all of the Black Ooze covering the bubble-sphere assuming that each puffer could eat at least 3 ounces of it in one minute?* He glanced at the clock on the classroom wall. Just 5 more minutes to go.

Ms. Shanti stood up from behind her desk and made her way over towards the door. Mark watched curiously as she slowly pulled down the shade and proceeded to lock the door.

"Miss. Shanti, eh, what are you doing?" Mark asked.

She walked over to him, stood directly in front of his desk, and smiled at him.

"So, tell me, Mark Tanner, how many puffers does it take to remove all of the Black Ooze from the surface of the bubble-sphere?"

"Hey! How did you know what I was...?" Mark stammered.

There was a sudden flash of blue light and there stood...Nadee, the Royal Princess of Mindar!

"NADEE!!" Mark exclaimed and he jumped up from his desk and pulled her tightly to him. About 5 seconds later he somewhat awkwardly pulled himself away from her.

"Uh, sorry about that. It's just that I'm, eh, really surprised to see you here."

"Don't be sorry, Mark," and she smiled warmly at him.

"So, what are you doing here? I haven't told anyone about Mindar! I swear!" Mark said firmly.

"I know you haven't. We are here for another reason," she replied.

"We?" Mark questioned and he looked around the room.

"Madison brought me here and she is now waiting for us at the beach," she explained to him.

"How's ol' Madison doing these days?" Mark asked her.

"She is good, but she does NOT like to be kept waiting, so we should be leaving now," Nadee said firmly.

"I will explain everything to you on the way to your home," she said.

"But..." Mark said.

"Just trust me, Mark," and she smiled at him.

As she reached for the door Mark put his hand on hers to stop her from opening it.

"Hey! Wait a minute. Don't you need to change back to your Miss Shanti look?" Mark asked.

"No! That will not be necessary!" she replied.

"Why not?" he asked her, feeling a little confused.

"Because, as of this very moment, I have officially retired from teaching," and she gave him a playful wink.

Then she opened the door, smiled, and said to him, "Shall we?"

As they began to navigate their way down the hallway Mark's mind was spinning like crazy. He had been wishing, hoping, even praying for this moment to come. But now that it was actually here, it had completely taken him by surprise. Here was the girl of his dreams very calmly walking along side of him down his school's hallway.

They quickly reached the school parking lot and headed in the direction of the Mustang. Some of his classmates had gathered around the car and were whispering amongst themselves.

Mark searched for the keys in his front pants pocket as they drew closer to the car.

"This is your ride!?!" the Princess' eyes widened. "It is a wondrous shade of blue!"

Mark opened the door for her, she thanked him, and he watched as she climbed into the car.

"Hot car, hot girl! You're movin' up in the world, Tanner," one of his classmates remarked.

At the turn of a key the Mustang roared to life.

As they made their way towards the Tanner house Mark kept sneaking glances over at Nadee.

"You would do well to keep your eyes on the road in front of you and NOT on me!" she teased. Mark blushed noticeably.

"So, you said you were going to tell me why you and Madison are here," Mark said to her. "Is Mindar okay? Did Ka-Lan come back?" he asked with concern.

"Mindar is perfectly fine, Mark, and we are quite confident that we have seen the last of the wizard."

"So, if the city's okay, and it's got nothing to do with Ka-Lan...then, why are you here?"

"I am here to invite you," she replied.

"Invite me!?! To what?" Mark asked.

"Last night when we talked, I could tell how disappointed you were about your mom not being able to attend your graduation ceremony."

"Yeah, I'm sorry about that. I didn't do a very good job of hiding it, did I?" he said softly.

"After we finished talking, I suggested something to Madison and she was able to gain the Council's approval," Nadee said.

"Approval of what, Nadee?" Mark asked her.

"The people of Mindar would like to throw you a graduation party, Mark!" she said excitedly.

"Seriously!?! They wanna' throw a party for me?!?" Mark exclaimed.

"Well, you and Sasper did help to save the entire city! Now, they see an opportunity to do something for you in return. It's a great way for them to say THANK YOU!"

"Madison and I are here to bring you and Sasper back to Mindar," Nadee told him.

"That would be totally awesome, Nadee!" But lemme' think about it for just a second here…"

"Okay! My mom's gonna' be out of town until Sunday night so that solves that problem, and Michael is home on his summer break from college, but I'm sure he won't be hanging around the house. I'm thinking this just might work," Mark said, and he smiled.

"…And you said Sasper is invited, too?" Mark asked.

"Yes! Sasper is always welcome in Mindar!" she replied.

"Well, then I say…LET'S DO IT!" Mark said happily.

"We thought you might like to drop by your home and get a few things to bring with you, and we can pick up Sasper, too," she advised him.

"Man. he's gonna' totally flip out! We're going back to Mindar!" Mark exclaimed.

"Hey! I was just thinking…there's a place that I'd like to take you to before we head down there."

"Oh, what do you have in mind, Mark?" the undersea princess asked.

"TRUST ME!" and Mark winked at her.

"I must ask Madison first to make sure that it's okay," Nadee said.

The dark-haired girl closed her eyes for a moment and then she quickly re-opened them. "Madison said yes," she said happily.

"COOL!" Mark said.

Just a short time later, Mark pulled the Mustang into the parking area for Les' Sundae Shop.

"Okay! Here we are," Mark said with a big grin.

Nadee looked up at the sign and asked, "Who is this Les that the sign speaks of?"

"I honestly don't know. I've never actually met the guy in person, but he absolutely has the BEST ice cream in town!"

"Ice cream!?! What is...ice cream?" Nadee questioned.

"You'll see," and they quickly headed for the open window to place an order.

"We'll have 2 vanilla cones with chocolate sprinkles, please," Mark said to the girl inside.

A few minutes later they were each holding a vanilla ice cream cone in their hands.

Mark spied an open table off to their left and they headed for it, "Come on, we can sit over there."

Mark eagerly began to lick his ice cream cone and he motioned to Nadee to join him. She leaned in and took her first lick of the vanilla cone that she was holding. Her eyes widened!

"This is...DELICIOUS!! I LOVE ICE CREAM!!" she said very excitedly.

"NOT surprised...most people do," and Mark laughed out loud.

"What are those small brown things on the top?" she asked.

"Those are called chocolate sprinkles. They come in a rainbow-flavor, too," he replied.

Nadee then proceeded to "attack" her ice cream cone and she succeeded in getting quite a bit of it on her face in the process. Mark leaned over and gently dabbed her face with a wet napkin. Nadee smiled appreciatively at him.

"Well, that cone sure DIDN'T stand a chance!" and he laughed out loud.

Nadee threw her head back and laughed. "NO! IT DID NOT! And neither will the next one!!" she shouted.

"So, are you happy that we stopped here?" Mark asked.

"VERY HAPPY!" she quickly answered. "I will always remember the wonderful day that I discovered...ICE CREAM!"

"COOL! Well, let me buy you one more and then we'll head for my house."

A few moments later, they were back on the road again.

As Mark turned the corner of Maple Street and his house came into view, the happy look on his face changed to one of concern. Parked in the driveway was his brother's candy apple red Chevelle and he had chosen today to wash his car.

"Seriously!?!" Mark muttered under his breath.

Mark leaned over and he whispered to Nadee, "Okay! Things could get a little tricky here."

"What do you mean...tricky?" she asked him.

"I wasn't expecting Michael to be here. I was going to just leave him a note saying that I was going to be spending some time at a friend's house. Now, knowing him, he's gonna' ask us

25

a whole bunch of stupid questions. We don't have time for this and Madison's waiting for us down at the beach."

"So, what do we do, Mark?" Nadee asked.

"You just follow my lead, and I think we'll be okay," he said to her. The Royal Princess of Mindar nodded.

As they neared the house, Mark called out to Michael, "She's lookin' real good, bro'!"

"Thanks, man," Michael replied, and he looked up from sudsing down his car.

Michael's eyes immediately fell on Nadee and he said, "...And speaking of things lookin' good.... who's the pretty lady, bro'?"

"This is my, eh, friend, Nadee," Mark answered.

"Your friend, huh? So, where you from, beautiful?" Mark's older brother asked.

"She's from...out of town," Mark quickly answered.

"Oh? Where out of town? What city do you live in?" Michael asked.

"She lives in..." Mark started to say, but Michael interrupted him.

"I'm asking her, bro'...NOT you!" he said firmly.

"I live in a wondrous city far away from here," Nadee replied.

"Wondrous, huh?" and Michael chuckled to himself.

"It's a really small town. You've probably never even heard of it," Mark said.

"So, how'd you guys' hook-up?" Michael asked.

"We met online a few months ago," Mark answered him.

"Doesn't he ever let you talk?" Michael asked and he looked directly at Nadee.

"So, what do you do for work, Nadee from a really small town that I've probably never heard of?"

"I DO NOT work! I am a Royal Princess," Nadee said proudly.

Michael's eyes lit up as if he'd just hit the lottery! Here was a golden opportunity to have some fun giving Mark a hard time.

"You don't say. So, you're a real-life princess, huh?" Michael teased.

"Yes, and my undersea kingdom is..."

"HA! ...And she has her very own undersea kingdom, too!" and Michael laughed out loud.

"You doubt my word, Michael Tanner?" Nadee said, and she took a step towards him.

Seeing the look in her eyes and hearing the tone in her voice, Mark quickly stepped between the two of them. "Nadee...NO!" Mark yelled.

What followed next was about twenty seconds of awkward silence. Then, Michael threw back his head and laughed out loud.

"She's all yours, man!" and he slapped his younger brother on the shoulder.

"She's got a lil' snarl to her, too...I like it!"

Michael then turned and jumped into his Chevelle and placed the key in the ignition.

As he was pulling out of the driveway, he just couldn't resist taking one final jab at Mark, "Now, you two just go and enjoy your little undersea kingdom together!" and he howled with laughter as the red Chevelle quickly sped away.

Mark and Nadee stood there silently watching Michael's car as it headed down Maple Street.

Nadee turned to Mark and said, "Your brother is MOST fortunate. I have defeated many much larger than him," she said firmly.

"Listen, I know you could've taken him out pretty easily but beating up my brother doesn't make for a very good first impression."

"...And what's with all this...I'm a royal princess under the sea stuff? I thought we were supposed to be keeping everything a big secret!" Mark challenged her.

"Your brother PROVOKED me. NONE are allowed to speak to me in such a manner! I am a Royal Princess, and I will be treated as such!" Nadee said, her dark eyes flashing.

"I hear ya'. Just remind me to never get on your bad side, okay?" Mark said and he smiled.

"C'mon. Let's get Sasper, grab some of my stuff, and get outta' here before anything else happens."

As they entered the Tanner family's house Nadee's eyes widened. "You live here!?! It is a royal palace!" she exclaimed.

"My mom would appreciate hearing you say that. She's tried very hard to make this place a good home for us," Mark shared. "...And it hasn't been easy on her with my dad gone," he added.

"Do you miss him?" Nadee asked.

"Everyday!" Mark said softly.

As they continued to make their way through the house, something white suddenly streaked across the upstairs carpet. Without any warning, it launched itself directly at them from the top of the stairs.

Nadee caught Sasper safely in her arms, and approximately twenty-seven very appreciative licks later, Nadee, the Royal Princess of Mindar, and Sasper the Wonder Dog, had now been officially reacquainted with each other.

"Well, somebody's sure happy to see you again," Mark said to her.

"...And I am very happy to see him, as well," and she held him tightly in her arms.

Mark then addressed Sasper, "Okay! So, here's the deal, bud."

Sasper's ears immediately went straight up as he listened to his best friend.

"Mindar has decided to throw a big party to help me celebrate my graduating from high school, and they've invited both of us! So, what do you say, bud? Ya' wanna' go spend some time in Mindar?"

Sasper started barking like crazy and jumping up and down leaving no doubt as to his answer.

"I'd say that's a definite yes!" and Mark laughed.

Mark then grabbed a pen and some paper and wrote a quick note to Michael saying that he was going out of town, but that he'd be back before his graduation ceremony.

"Okay! That should do it," Mark said to Nadee.

A quick shower...some freshly washed clothes stuffed in a duffle bag...a few doggie treats for Sasper to enjoy on the trip down...and it was time for them to leave.

"Madison, we are ready!" the undersea princess shouted.

A familiar blue-energy quickly entered the living room, and it completely enveloped them. Then, just like that, they were gone.

~ Never Mess with a Princess ~

They quickly reappeared on the same secluded stretch of Folly Beach as the last time.

"Okay! Now, let's find Madison and..." Mark started to say.

"Well, well, and what do we have here?" a deep male voice came from somewhere behind them.

As they turned around, they saw three young men staring back at them.

"Look, man. We don't want any trouble here," Mark said to the one standing in front.

"Well, that's really too bad, bro', cuz' it looks like trouble just found...YOU!!" he snarled.

Sasper growled loudly at them, and Mark quickly reached for his collar to hold him back.

"Better keep your mutt under control or he's gonna' get hurt bad!" one of them said.

"Today is collection day, boys an' girls! And since you're trespassing on our beach..."

"It's NOT your beach! This is a public beach!" Mark fired back at them.

"NOT today it isn't, so just hand over your wallet and we'll just be on our way!"

Mark whispered to Nadee, "This is about to get really ugly," and he stepped out in front of her.

The Royal Princess of Mindar, however, had some ideas of her own. With a perfectly executed back-flip over Mark's head, she landed right in the middle of the three would-be-assailants.

What happened next was almost too fast for the human eye to follow. Some two minutes later and the 3 young men were all lying in the sand holding onto various body parts and howling in tremendous pain.

"LEAVE...WHILE YOU STILL CAN!!" the dark-haired girl commanded them.

Mark, Nadee, and Sasper watched as they struggled to get to their feet and then limped away. As they left, they were shaking their heads and probably asking themselves the question...*what just happened?!?*

ANSWER: They had picked the *wrong* princess to mess with!

"C'mon. Let's get outta' here before they decide to come back," Mark advised them.

"They WILL NOT return!" Nadee said firmly.

"How can you be so sure, Nadee?" Mark asked her.

"Because I *broke* one of them!" and she smiled at him.

"You *broke* one of them?!?" Mark repeated her words.

"That was...FUN!" and she gave him a playful wink.

"You think that was fun, huh?" and he just looked at her. "You were...AMAZING!" Mark said in clear admiration.

"Well, Talena and I have been practicing some new fighting moves. This was the perfect opportunity to try some of them out," Nadee shared.

Sasper then decided to add a few appreciative barks of his own.

"C'mon, let's go find Madison before something else crazy happens to us," Mark advised.

The three young adventurers quickly made their way to the water's edge, and they began to scan the surface of the water for the arrival of their shape-shifting friend. A few seconds later Madison surfaced, and she began to make her way towards the shoreline.

"Hey! You just missed all of the excitement!" Mark shouted at her.

"Saw the whole thing! You guys weren't in any real danger or I woulda' stepped in. Maybe those punks will think twice the next time!" Madison shouted across the waves.

"Alright, our time's a wastin' here...Let's head for Mindar," Madison urged them.

Nadee, Mark and Sasper phased into Madison and then she headed for the open sea. Mark and Sasper took one last good look at the beach.

"We're going back to Mindar, bud!" Mark said excitedly to Sasper.

The little white dog looked up and let out a shrill bark. A low-flying flock of pelicans flew by overhead just as Madison dipped below the ocean waves.

~ Mindar's Heroes Remembered ~

As Madison began her descent towards the ocean floor, Mark turned to Nadee and said, "I want to thank you for doing this for me, Nadee. I really appreciate it."

"You saved my entire city, Mark! Now, we can do something in return for you."

"Hey! Saving the day is our *thing*, Princess," Sasper added.

"Dude, you can talk again! So, how's it feel?" Mark asked his furry friend.

"Pretty spiffy, bro'!" Sasper replied.

"Spiffy!?!" and Mark laughed out loud.

Mark and Sasper moved closer to Madison's outer wall so they could get a better look at things. A wave of sheer excitement washed over them. The undersea world all around them was so BEAUTIFUL!

For so long they had wanted to return to Mindar and now it was finally happening. But this time the circumstances of their trip below were completely different. This time there was NO evil wizard bent on world conquest for them to deal with. No! This visit was all about celebrating a wonderful moment in Mark's life.

The sound of the undersea princess' voice interrupted Mark's thoughts.

"Once we're back in Mindar there is something that I want you both to see. It is something that I think you will like very much," Nadee said, and she smiled at them.

"Well, we can't wait to see it then," Mark replied.

"What he said, Princess!" Sasper added.

It wasn't long before the great Silver Dome that encloses the city of Mindar came into view. Madison and her three passengers quickly phased through it and appeared on the other side.

Geren, as always, was right there to greet them.

"Welcome back, land-walkers!" he said to them with a big smile.

"Great to see you, Geren?" Mark said.

"How's the Mrs. doin'?" Sasper asked.

"She is fine. I will tell her that you asked about her," Geren answered.

"You do that!" Sasper replied.

With another *blink* they found themselves standing in the center of Mindar.

A huge crowd had gathered there to welcome them back. They were holding up signs that read, *"Happy Graduation Day!"* and *"Congratulations, Mark!"* The huge crowd then began to chant Mark's name over and over again.

Sasper whispered to Mark, "Dude, you're like a rockstar here!"

Mark smiled appreciatively and waved to the crowd.

The group began to make its way down Main Street and in the direction of the castle.

"Hey! Look down, bro. Check out what's under us," Sasper advised.

Mark looked down and his eyes widened at what he saw. The entire street was made up of beautiful seashells!

"INCREDIBLE!" was all Mark could think of saying.

"It's like the Yellowbrick Road in *"The Wizard of Oz"*... only undersea-style!" Sasper exclaimed. "But this one's made outta' gorgeous seashells!" he added.

As they rounded the corner, they saw what Nadee had mentioned earlier to them on the ride down. Large statues made of bronze had been erected in their honor in the very heart of the city.

Mark's statue featured him sitting on Adventurer and holding his battle sword high. Sasper's statue depicted him riding on the back of Blue the dolphin and holding the silver sphere up in his right paw. There were also statues of the Royal Princess of Mindar swinging her battle-stick and one of Madison, as well...and finally, there was a bronze statue of the mighty warrior Brom swinging his battle sword.

"I'm really glad they made one of Brom," Mark said, and he smiled remembering his friend.

"He stood with us at the very end. He should be remembered that way," Madison said firmly.

"I think this would make him very happy," Mark offered.

As they were about to enter the Royal Castle, Nadee turned to face the crowd.

"Tonight, we will gather in the Great Banquet Hall to celebrate Mark's high school graduation!" she shouted.

The crowd cheered wildly.

Mark looked down at Sasper and whispered, "This is CRAZY! All this just for me??"

"Hey! Enjoy your moment in the sun, bud!" Sasper encouraged his friend.

As they entered the Royal Castle, Mark turned to Nadee, "So, what do we do until tonight?"

"Oh, I have something in mind that I think you both will like," and she smiled. "But first things first..."

Talena appeared and she smiled at Mark and Sasper, "Welcome back, cool dudes!"

"It's great to be back, Talena," Mark said to her.

"So, how ya' doin', T?" Sasper asked the pretty blonde-haired girl.

"Doin' just fine! Alright, let's get you two settled into your room," she replied.

"Just give me your *ten digits* and we'll blink on outta' here!" Talena advised them.

~ Jacuzzi Time! ~

A *blink* later and Mark and Sasper were standing in the guest room they had stayed in the last time they were in Mindar.

Sasper's eyes widened, and he made a beeline straight for the large round bed in the far corner of the guest room.

"ALL MINE!!" he shouted with gusto, and he began to happily roll all over the bed.

"You can do that later, bro'. We need to get cleaned up now," Mark reminded him.

"Okay! But just give me another 2 minutes here... please...please..." Sasper begged him.

"Alright...2 minutes! ...And NOT one second more!" Mark commanded. "I'm gonna' take a quick shower and you better be ready when I get back out here!" he warned.

Mark then turned and headed for the bathroom.

As he was enjoying the relaxing hot shower, Mark was suddenly surprised to hear someone singing very loudly.

"What the?!?" and he quickly wrapped a towel around his waist and went in search of the sound.

When he entered the room what he saw was just too ridiculous for him to even try and put into words and he immediately burst out laughing.

There was Sasper sitting right in the middle of the room in a small jacuzzi! He was holding up a gold hairbrush to his mouth and singing..."Who Let The Dogs Out!"

"Seriously, dude!?!" Mark exclaimed.

The little white dog just looked over at him and grinned. "You jealous of my amazing singing voice?" he asked coyly.

"Not really," Mark replied. "But since when do you like baths of any kind?" Mark questioned. "Back home you always run and hide under the bed whenever mom says its bath time."

"It's NOT a bath, bro'! It's a JACUZZI! We're talkin' a completely different animal here. But if you really must know, it soooooothes me!" and the little white dog sighed deeply.

"Yeah, well, Nadee's comin' to get us any minute now so, you just go right ahead and get your sooooothed furry butt outta' there!!" Mark shouted.

"Hey! I always need to look my best, bro'! I'm gonna' be on the cover of "DQ" someday!" Sasper said quite confidently.

"DQ, huh? Never heard of it," Mark said.

"Dogs Quarterly, dude! Seriously, it's Big-Time!"

"What are you living in a cave somewhere?" Sasper said loudly.

"Well, just get finished up here, will ya'?" Mark urged him.

"You got it, bro'!" the little white dog replied with a happy smile.

~ The Big Question ~

Very shortly, there was a gentle knock on the door to the guest room.

When Mark opened it there stood the beautiful Royal Princess of Mindar.

"Are you two ready to go?" she asked.

"Yup! We're all set," Mark quickly answered her.

A quick blink and they were once again standing near the Royal Stables.

"Come with me," and the Princess motioned for them to follow her.

They climbed up the steps to a large white house and watched as Nadee gently knocked on the door. Nothing could have prepared them for what they were about to see. As the door opened wide before them, there stood their giant-fisted friend...BUNDAR! Only, he was dressed in a ultra-skin-tight purple wrestling costume and wearing a pair of bright yellow boots!

"Bundar?!? Is that really you??" and the Princess giggled uncontrollably.

Bundar then lifted up his purple mask just slightly with his right hand and said, "Please, forgive me, my Princess! I was told that you would be coming by sometime later," Bundar stammered.

"I most definitely believe you, my old friend!" and she laughed out loud.

Bundar looked at Mark and Sasper and said, "Welcome back to Mindar, my friends," and he held out his huge right hand.

"Great to see you again, Bundar!" Mark said happily.

Bundar then leaned down to shake Sasper's paw. "Put 'er there, my furry friend!" Bundar said with a big smile on his face.

"It's good to see, you, too, *red*!" Sasper replied. "So, what's with the crazy get-up, dude?" Sasper asked Bundar.

"This is my new wrestling costume," Bundar replied proudly. "I call myself...*The Purple Hammer*," and he threw back his head, put his hands on his hips, and stuck his chest out just as far as it could possibly go.

"The Purple Hammer, huh? I like it!" Mark said.

"...And what do you think of my wrestling costume, Princess?" Bundar asked hopefully.

"Well, it is quite colorful, my friend!" Nadee offered.

"Well, since you're here now, you may as well ride," the huge, red-bearded man said.

"I will go and get Adventurer and Indy for you at once, my Princess. They were both absolutely thrilled to learn that their friends from above were returning to Mindar," he added.

"Wait here for just a moment, please," and he turned and quickly headed for the corral.

As the 2 huge seahorses came into view, Adventurer shouted at Mark, "Ola, mi amigo!"

"Hey, Adventurer! It's great to see you again, bud! You, too, Indy!" Mark shouted back.

"...And you and Sasper, as well," Indy replied, and she smiled warmly at them.

41

As they drew closer, Mark asked, "So, how's married life treating you two?"

"It is a gran aventura and I have the perfect companion to share it with," Adventurer shared happily.

"Thank you, my love. But...he DOES snore quite loudly at night when we are trying to sleep!" Indy revealed.

"INDY!! That is simply NOT true!" Adventurer said very adamantly.

"It is just a false rumor, my sweet one!" he added.

"Well, then it's a VERY loud rumor every night, my love," and the beautiful pearl grey seahorse gave him a playful wink.

"Well, this one here...she steals all of the covers away from me in the middle of the night!" Adventurer protested loudly.

"You are mistaken, my love. I do NO such thing!" Indy teased.

Mark looked over at Sasper and he whispered to him, "Yup! DEFINITELY married!!"

"Most DEFINITELY!!" Sasper whispered back and he snickered.

Mark placed his foot in the golden stirrup and pulled himself up and over. Then he slid down directly into the waiting golden saddle in the middle of Adventurer's back.

He leaned over and put his arms around Adventurer's neck and held him tightly.

"I've really missed ya' buddy!" Mark said happily.

"...And I have missed you, too, my young friend!" Adventurer replied.

Sasper looked around and said, "Hey! Where's Blue?"

A voice came from somewhere behind the small white dog, "I'm right here, dude!"

"Cool!" Sasper exclaimed, and he quickly leaped up onto Blue's back and grabbed ahold of the dorsal fin of his friend.

"Man, it's great to see you!" Sasper said.

"Same here, dude!" the blue dolphin replied.

"So, how ya' been, bud?" Sasper asked Blue.

"Livin' the good life! Being one of Mindar's heroes is a pretty cool thing!" he replied.

"I believe we are now ready to ride, Bundar," the Princess stated.

"Alright, then! Have fun, everyone!" and Bundar turned and headed in the direction of his house.

As the happily reunited group made their way steadily across the ocean floor, there were plenty of things for them to talk about.

"So, how's Zarden doing these days?" Mark asked.

"Yeah, when do we get to see our all-time favorite sea dragon?" Sasper asked.

"He will be joining us tonight at the party," Adventurer shared with them.

"For now, he is...resting!" and Indy laughed out loud.

"Z's sleeping?" Sasper questioned sounding a little surprised.

"Si, I'm afraid our playful lil' ninos completely wore him out last night!" Adventurer said.

"Ninos?!? You mean kids??" Mark asked Adventurer.

"Si. We have hundreds of lil' ones to be looked after and he makes a wonderful baby-sitter," Adventurer shared.

"NO WAY! Z...babysits?" Sasper exclaimed.

"Si, Sasper! They all love him mucho!" and Adventurer smiled.

"He has a special way with them," Indy added.

"I'm tryin' to picture our boy Z as a baby-sitter," and Sasper laughed at the very idea.

As they continued to make their way across the ocean floor, Mark couldn't help but smile. Everything about his being here just felt so...RIGHT! He was with Nadee and her wonderful undersea friends exploring the incredible beauty that was all around him. Something seemed to be speaking to him and it was saying...STAY! This is where you truly belong! But could his dream somehow become a reality?

After a while, Mark became rather quiet, and Nadee noticed it. Sasper picked up on it, too, and he decided to give his long-time friend a little space.

"Blue and I are gonna' cruise on over that way and see what we can find," he announced. "We'll catch up with you guys in a little while."

"Sounds good!" Mark said.

As they watched Sasper and Blue disappear somewhere into the ocean depths, Nadee turned to Mark and said, "So, why are you so quiet, Mark?" she asked softly. "Are you not happy to have returned?" she sounded concerned.

"I'm very HAPPY!" Mark said and he smiled at her.

Then he looked directly into her eyes, and he said to her, "I was just wondering... do you ever miss your family and your island home?"

She thought for a long moment before answering him.

"Yes, there are moments when I do miss them terribly. But then I realize that I have created a wonderful new life for myself here in Mindar. This is now...MY HOME!" and she smiled.

"It does help that my family is still within reach if I should ever wish to visit them," she added.

Nadee's family and many of her friends had returned home to the island of Peninda several months ago. They were instructed to say nothing about the underwater city of Mindar. Since the island of Peninda was so isolated from the rest of the world, there would be little chance of anyone ever accidentally giving away any of Mindar's secrets.

Mark's situation was, of course, quite the opposite of that. The city of Charleston, South Carolina was incredibly popular, and it welcomed millions of visitors every year from all over the world. That was the single biggest reason that Madison could NOT allow Mark to visit Nadee whenever he wanted to.

"Why are you asking me this, Mark?" she asked him.

"Just...thinking...about things," he replied.

Nadee looked at him and said, "There are many wonderful places in this world that you could be, but you must be in the one place that speaks the strongest to your own heart, Mark. It is a decision that you alone must make at some point! NO ONE can make it for you, nor would you ever want them to. THE CHOICE MUST BE YOURS!"

"I know that, and you're right, Nadee," Mark replied.

Nadee sat up in her saddle and looked around for Sasper and Blue.

"We should be heading back. We need to get ready for tonight's celebration," she said.

As if right on cue, Sasper and Blue suddenly appeared and they quickly rejoined them.

As the Royal Stables came into their view, Adventurer said, "Princess, I would like to speak to Mark alone for a few minutes, por favor?"

"Of course. We'll wait for you over there," and she pointed at the corral.

Mark and Adventurer watched as the others slowly moved away from them.

"What's up, bud?" Mark asked the majestic black seahorse.

"You must tell her, mi amigo!" he said firmly.

"You mean, Nadee? Oh yeah, I forgot that you're inside of my head," Mark said to him.

"Si! I know your thoughts and that is why I am telling you this," he said.

"Then, you know why I'm having such a hard time with this. If I choose to stay here with her does that mean I have to say goodbye to my family? ...And I don't even know for sure how she really feels about me," Mark said.

"Si, I understand, mi amigo. But you must find out how she truly feels about you before any other decisions can be made," Adventurer stated.

"Yeah, that makes sense," Mark agreed. "But when should I talk to her?" he asked his friend.

"You must wait for just the right moment," Adventurer advised him.

"I don't suppose you already know how she feels about me, do you?" Mark asked.

"Even if I did know, I would NOT tell you. This is just between the two of you, mi amigo."

"Alright, I'll do it. I'll make sure I talk to her before I go back home," Mark said to Adventurer. "...And thanks for the great advice, bud."

"No problemo!" Adventurer replied.

Mark and Adventurer rejoined the others who were waiting for them patiently by the corral.

"Tonight, we will celebrate, my friends!" Adventurer called out as he turned to leave with Indy.

"Later, dude!" Sasper replied.

~ Time to Celebrate ~

A quick blink later, Mark and Sasper were once again standing in the guest room.

"I will send Talena to get you," Nadee said to them.

Sasper looked up at Mark and gave him a gentle tug on his pants leg.

"Nadee, I..." Mark began.

"Yes, Mark?" the beautiful, dark-haired girl replied.

"Uh, what should we wear for this thing?" Mark asked.

"It's your night so wear whatever you want to," and she smiled at him.

"Okay! Got it!" Mark answered.

"We'll see you later then," Mark said to her.

"I am glad that you have returned to Mindar," the undersea princess said, and she headed for the door.

"Yeah, me, too," and he smiled at her.

Mark closed the door and stood there for a moment.

"Couldn't do it, could ya'?" Sasper said to his friend.

"It just...didn't feel right," Mark replied. "Maybe I'll do it tonight,"

"So, what did Adventurer want to talk to you about?" Sasper asked.

"He said that I needed to talk to Nadee and find out how she really feels about me," Mark responded.

"He's right! You can't live in two worlds, bro'! It just CAN'T be done!" Sasper said firmly.

"It's time to find out where you stand with her!" Sasper added.

"I'm...scared!" Mark said softly.

"Hey, I'd be scared, too, bro'!" Sasper said.

"Facing Brom in the arena was less scary than this," Mark offered.

"What if she doesn't..." Mark started to say.

"What IFs will drive you crazy, bud!" Sasper said.

"Besides, no matter what she says, you've still got me and my wonderful singing voice," and Sasper laughed.

"DON'T quit your day job, bro'!" and Mark laughed.

"Alright, let's get ready for tonight, and thanks for being there for me. I really appreciate it!" Mark said.

"Anytime, bro'," Sasper answered.

Later that night, as Mark and Sasper entered the Great Banquet Hall, they were greeted with a thunderous roar! A sea of happy faces...citizens of Mindar and sea-dwellers alike...filled the room to overflowing.

Nadee was already seated at the head table along with Madison and Zarden.

Mark and Sasper followed Talena to the front of the room and then they sat down at the head table.

The first real surprise of the night came when Mark and Sasper noticed a very familiar face on the podium.

"KING CRAB!!" Mark shouted. "What are you doing here, Your Majesty?"

"They asked me to be the MC for tonight's festivities and, of course, I was delighted to do it," he replied.

"Lookin' good, Your Majesty!" Sasper said loudly.

"...And you, as well, Sasper. Tell me, are you enjoying the bone that we gave you"?

"Most definitely! It's the MOST delicious thing I've ever tasted!" the little white dog answered him.

"That pleases me greatly!" the royal undersea monarch said.

King Crab looked out at the huge, assembled crowd and said, "Well, now that you are here, I believe it's time to get this party started!"

"My fellow sea-dwellers and noble Mindarians... WELCOME!" King Crab said loudly.

"We are gathered here tonight to say...THANK YOU...to someone who risked everything for us! ...And to also share a very special moment in their life with them!"

King Crab then looked over at Mark and said, "Mark, will you please join me at the podium."

Mark stood up and quickly made his way over to the podium.

"Our young friend here is now graduating from high school!" King Crab bellowed.

There was a loud round of applause from the gathered crowd.

"Mark, would you like to say a few words?" King Crab asked.

50

The room became very hushed.

Mark began to speak... "I'm really not sure what to say right now. I just want all of you to know that, well, you doing this for me...it means a lot to me...and I'll NEVER forget it...EVER!"

The crowd of Mindarians and sea-dwellers began to chant... "Mark...Mark...Mark."

Mark waved his hand to quiet the crowd.

"Wherever I am, I want you to know that I will always consider myself to be a Mindarian! THANK YOU EVERYONE!!" Mark shouted.

Mark returned to the head table to the sound of applause and sat back down.

"Well said, kid," Madison whispered to him.

Nadee simply smiled.

King Crab then addressed the crowd again, "Alright, everyone! It's...PARTY-TIME!! ENJOY YOURSELVES!"

Throughout the night, Mindarians and sea-dwellers alike came by to offer Mark their congratulations and their best wishes for his future.

Out of the corner of his eye, Mark noticed Lt. Tallus moving very quickly towards their table. Everyone noticed the look of concern on the young lieutenant's face.

"My Princess...I am very sorry for the intrusion, but..." Lt. Tallus began.

"Yes, what is it?" she asked him.

"We have just received an urgent communication from Zarden's mother. She wishes to speak with him immediately."

Zarden exclaimed, "My mother...? I will follow you," and he quickly left the hall with the young lieutenant.

Everyone watched with great concern as their friend left the Great Banquet Hall.

"I sure hope everything is okay," Mark said.

"Somethin's wrong! I can feel it in my bones, guys!" Sasper shared.

"My life-spirit senses it, too, Sasper," the Princess said.

"We should go be with Zarden now," she suggested.

She then got up from the table and the others did the same. They made their way over to the communications center. As they were just about to go inside, Zarden was on his way out. The worried look on his face told them everything that they needed to know.

"My friends..." Zarden addressed them.

"Has something happened back home?" Nadee asked.

"My father has fallen very ill. My mother feels that we may lose him and..." his voice trailed off and he began to cry.

Nadee immediately stepped forward and put her arms around her friend's neck.

"Is there anything that can be done for him?" she asked.

"I will be leaving immediately to go and be with my family," Zarden shared.

"Then, we're going with you, bud!" Mark said loudly.

"You heard 'em, big guy!" Sasper added.

"I will go with you, as well," the Princess said, and she smiled at Zarden.

"Well, I guess it's unanimous then!" Madison said.

Zarden looked at his friends and said, "NO! I CANNOT allow you to do this! It is much too DANGEROUS! There is NO guarantee that you will return here safely!" The great sea dragon warned.

"Hey! Danger is my middle name, dude! Ya' know, I kinda' like that...Sasper Tanner...Danger Dog!" and he threw back his head and howled.

"Friends are always there for each other! We're going!!" Mark said firmly.

Seeing that their minds were made up, Zarden simply nodded.

"I am most fortunate to have all of you as my friends!" and he smiled at them, fighting back the tears in his eyes.

"Alright, time's a wastin' here...everyone, get yur' stuff together cuz' we're outta' here in twenty minutes!" Madison instructed them.

Mark closed his eyes and said, " I need a piece of paper, a pen, and a glass bottle, please!"

"Whatcha' doin', bud?" Sasper asked.

Instantly, a piece of white paper, a pen, and a glass bottle appeared on a nearby table.

"I want to write a note to my family, just in case we don't..."

"I get it..." Sasper said to him.

A few minutes later, Mark was ready to place the piece of paper in the glass bottle.

"Hey! Hold up a sec...," Sasper requested.

Sasper closed his eyes and said loudly, "I need some black ink here, please!"

Instantly, a small bottle of black ink appeared, and Sasper carefully poured it over his right paw. Then, he pressed down hard with his little white paw on the paper.

"DONE!" he said.

Mark nodded, rolled up the piece of paper, and slid it into the glass bottle.

"Talena, if we don't make it back here, then I want you to..." Mark said to her.

"You two are COMIN' BACK!" she said loudly, then she hugged them both.

"Okay! We'll be right back," Mark said, and they blinked back to the guestroom.

Nadee turned to Talena, who was starting to cry. "Talena, I..."

Talena threw her arms around Nadee and held her tight.

"Come back safe, my sister!" she whispered.

"I WILL!" the undersea princess said firmly.

Then Nadee blinked from the room saying, "I will return shortly."

As they reappeared in the room, there was a very determined look on all of their faces.

"Alright, boys an' girls. Let's move!" Madison said very loudly.

~ Zarden's Tale ~

A blink later and they were standing just outside of the huge Silver Dome.

"If anyone's thinkin' about changin' their mind about goin'...now's the time for ya' ta' speak up," and one-by-one Madison scanned their faces.

"We're all in, Madison," Mark said firmly.

"Before we go, there is something I would like to say to everyone," the Princess said.

Everyone then gave their full attention to the Royal Princess of Mindar.

"My friends, I commend your bravery! We will do everything we possibly can to help our good friend Zarden and his family in their time of need."

"Well said, Princess," Madison stated.

They were about to "phase" into Madison and begin their journey when they heard a familiar voice from behind them.

"My friends...WAIT!"

Everyone turned to see four huge great white sharks now approaching them.

"ARTHUR!!" Mark shouted happily as he recognized his friend from Australia.

"Madison got word to us that you an' yur' friends are headin' down to the Dark Depths."

"Yeah, Zarden's dad is really sick, so we're going with him to try and help somehow," Mark said to Arthur.

"Well, my mates an' me want to help, too," Arthur said.

"How can you help, Arthur?" the Princess asked.

"By providin' ya' with protection for as long as we can, Princess," Arthur shared.

"Way ta' go, Sharkeys! No one's gonna' mess with us with you guys around to protect us!" Sasper said.

Mark then addressed the other three great white sharks saying, "Thanks, guys! We won't forget this."

The one to Arthur's left responded saying, "Arthur told us of how ya' helped him a while back with his bad tooth. Any friend of Arthur's is a friend of ours, mate!"

"We're glad ta' have you guys taggin' along with us," Madison said to them.

As they began to move away from the Silver Dome, Mark asked Madison, "Why don't you just use your super-speed to get us down there right away?"

"Can't do it, kid. There's tremendous water pressure at those depths. I can handle it just fine, but I'm NOT sure that you guys can!" Madison explained.

"So, yur' sayin' we have ta' take the slow boat to China on this one?" Sasper questioned.

"Unless ya' wanna' take a chance on us crackin' up like an eggshell!" Madison said.

"Yeah, we'll...PASS!" Mark stated.

"Will Zarden be alright in those depths?" the Princess asked with concern for her friend.

"He should be just fine. His body should readjust to the conditions on the way down," Madison explained.

"Alright, if there are no more questions...LET'S MOVE! Next stop...The Dark Depths!"

Madison then began her slow and steady descent to the ocean bottom, escorted by the four huge great white sharks.

"Hey! Check it out, dude. We've got our very own special escort! ONLY ours has a lot of really big teeth!" and Sasper laughed out loud.

After some time had passed, Madison addressed the group again.

"So, how's everybody doin', so far? Any problems that I should know about?" she asked.

"We are fine, Madison" the Princess answered her.

"Well, since this is gonna' take a while...anyone got any good stories to share to help pass the time?" Sasper asked.

Madison looked out at Zarden swimming alongside of the bubble-sphere, "How 'bout it, Z? You feel like tellin' 'em yur' story?"

The great sea dragon paused for a moment considering what to do next.

"It is something that I have rarely shared with anyone, but perhaps you should know my story," he said.

"Please, Zarden, tell us..." Nadee encouraged him.

"Very well, Princess," Zarden replied.

The great sea dragon of the deep then began to share with them.

"What I will now share with you happened in the far distant past. It will speak of family loyalties and of wonderful friendships, but it will also deal with painful sacrifice and terrible loss. In the end, it will have been a story about...SURVIVAL!"

"Long, long ago when the world was still very young my kind filled what you now call the Seven Seas. The vast ocean was our home. It was all we had ever known in our existence. It was a time when all lived in peace and harmony with each other. But life can change in a single heartbeat...and for us, sadly, it did!"

"The gift of a family is immeasurable, and I was very fortunate to have had mine. A wonderful mother and father who were always there for me to guide and instruct me. Their names were Zania and Zarak and I was their only child."

"I also had a great friend back then...his name was ZaMar. His mother and father, Zanee and Zern, were very good friends with my parents. ...And though we came from two different families, ZaMar and I always considered ourselves to be brothers. We vowed that NO matter what came our way in life it would never sever the strong bond that was between us. Be very careful in the words that you speak for sometimes they will be severely tested."

"I spoke earlier of change. It is quite foolish to think that everything will continue just as it always has. Sometimes things change for the better. Sometimes, things change for the worse. Time itself has always been the great revealer of all that is and all that will be. When change does come, there are those who will accept it gladly...there are those who accept it grudgingly and view it constantly with a suspicious eye...and those who will NEVER ever accept it!"

"One day, with absolutely no warning of any kind, everything suddenly changed for us! A new creature called "man" found his way into our world. At first, there were just a few of them, sailing across the seas in their fragile wooden ships. We observed them from a safe distance, admiring their courage and determined spirit."

"In the days that followed their numbers began to multiply dramatically! Occasionally, there would be an encounter of some kind between us. Fortunately, those tall sailor's tales were quickly dismissed by the leaders in their communities. But, with the number of their ships ever increasing, we knew that we could not remain hidden forever!"

"...And so, the Great Council convened for the specific purpose of deciding on what course of action, if any, should be taken. Our first cousins, the whales, also attended the meeting to have their voices heard, as well. My father believed that co-existence between us was entirely possible. Simply put, if we did NOT bother them, they would not bother us."

"ZaMar's father, Zern, strongly disagreed. After having observed men for years, he argued that they were combative by nature, and always seeking to conquer. A truly lasting peace of any kind always seemed to elude them. Zern argued that it was only a matter of time before we were discovered and then drawn into another one of their senseless conflicts."

"In the end, the Great Council sided with my father, and all those who believed as he did. ZaMar's father reluctantly agreed to abide by the council's decision, but he vowed to always remain vigilant. He, and those who thought as he did, would stand ever ready to do whatever was needed to protect our race."

"...And then, the "Day of Great Sadness" came! If I could, I would erase every memory from my mind of that tragic day. It started out just like so many other days, giving no hint of the horror that was to come."

"Zanee and Zern had decided to do a little exploring that day, something that they greatly enjoyed doing together. Somehow, they found themselves right in the middle of a small fleet of ships that was making its way towards the East coast. The five ships quickly began to encircle them, and a tremendous fear gripped their hearts. Escape was...IMPOSSIBLE!"

"Word came to us from other frightened sea-dwellers of what was now happening, and we immediately raced to help them in any way that we could. But as we came upon the scene, we knew that it was...TOO LATE! The conflict between our two races that we had tried so hard to avoid had already begun! Deadly harpoons fired from somewhere above us passed through the waters all around us. Some missed their intended targets, but sadly, others DID NOT miss!"

"As I looked up, I could see ZaMar's mother and father struggling mightily to free themselves from a great casting net. Slowly they were being pulled to the surface, where they would be completely helpless before their enemies. ZaMar was desperately trying to free them, tearing at the net with his sharp teeth, but the situation was hopeless."

I was close enough to hear Zern's last words to his son, *"You CAN'T save us, ZaMar! You must escape now, or you will share in our fate...GO!!"* *"I WON'T leave you!"* ZaMar screamed. *"YOU MUST GO, MY SON!!"* Zern shouted. *"We love you, ZaMar!!"* Zanee called out to him. ...And then, they were both GONE FOREVER!"

"Father...Mother..." the words fell from ZaMar's lips.

"ZaMar threw back his head and let out a terrible cry of anguish. Then, he turned away and he looked directly at me. The pain...the anger...I saw in his eyes on that day...I have NEVER once forgotten it!"

"There was a call to RETREAT! Those of us that were still alive heeded the call. Somehow, I was able to find my mother and father in the chaos surrounding me. We rejoiced that we had not lost our life-spirits like so many of our friends had. We quickly joined the other survivors in our group, and then we dove!"

"To escape was now our only thought! We went deeper...deeper...into the all-consuming darkness! There was NO light of any kind to be found anywhere. The sound of our voices served to keep us all together so that none were lost. The creatures we saw moving around us were quite strange in their appearance, covered as they were in brilliant lights."

"After what seemed like an eternity, we finally reached the bottom. In the time that followed we created a new home for ourselves on the ocean floor. Somehow, against all odds, we had managed to survive. But NOT everyone was ready to accept this new beginning for us. ZaMar and several others still carried a deep bitterness in their hearts for the loss of their loved ones. They especially blamed my father for having swayed the Great Council."

"In the end, the "outcasts", the name they chose for themselves, decided to leave us. I tried my best to convince ZaMar and his friends to stay, but he would NOT listen. He looked at me and with great anger in his voice said, *"We are brothers...NO MORE!!"* I watched very sadly as ZaMar and the other outcasts disappeared into the dark ocean depths.

"Many centuries later, it was decided that one of us should return to the world we had left behind to learn what had become of it, and to see if we could become part of it once more. I was...CHOSEN!"

"The day that I left I had so many mixed emotions running through me. I knew that I would miss my family terribly, but my mission was incredibly important. As I made my way to the surface, I could feel the water around me growing steadily warmer. My eyes kept adjusting to my new, much brighter surroundings. After having been in darkness for so long it felt absolutely...WONDERFUL! I remember the thrill of breaking the surface of the water and feeling once again the warmth of the sun. It was... GLORIOUS!"

"As I dove back below the surface of the water I was surprised to see other sea-dwellers. They had never seen one of my kind before and so they were quite fascinated with me. I told them why I had come and then I asked what had become of my cousins, the whales. Immediately, their eyes filled with deep sadness and showed great regret. Then, they shared with me one heart-breaking story after another. My great friends, these gentle giants of the deep, who bore absolutely NO ill will towards anyone, had been mercilessly hunted and killed to the very point of their extinction!"

I asked them, *"WHY??"* But NOT ONE among them could give me an answer. I CRIED!! The kind of crying that comes from a heart that has been truly broken. Then, my great pain turned into an uncontrollable rage! I would find a way to strike back at those who had done this evil to my friends. But I soon came to realize that it would be sheer folly to do so. I would be one against far too many with no chance at all."

"With a heavy heart, I made the decision to leave the surface world forever and return home. But before I returned, I would create a make-shift memorial so that my whale-friends would NEVER be forgotten. As I was gathering the things I needed, I chanced upon "Madison", who was out doing some undersea exploring of her own."

"I did not know at the time that it would be the beginning of a wonderful friendship that would last for many centuries. We talked for quite a while, and then she told me of the wondrous city of Mindar! A place where men and sea-dwellers lived together in perfect harmony with each other. After having heard so many tragic stories I must admit that I DID NOT believe her! Still, her words were quite convincing, and she encouraged me to come and *"see for myself,"* as she put it. ...And so, I did."

"I quickly discovered that everything Madison had told me was TRUE! The citizens of Mindar were very kind and welcoming to me. Of course, as you have now discovered for yourselves, the Mindarians have had more than their fair share of troubles over the many years. For one, the wizard Ka-Lan's aging-spell robbed Mindar of its great beauty and glory. ...And yet, these people never let bitterness take root in their hearts. Rather instead, they celebrated the gift of life itself and aways hoped for the best. It was truly... INSPIRING!"

"...And this led me to discover a very important truth! That in this world you will encounter those who do great good and those who do great evil. What is truly in their hearts will always be revealed at some point for everyone to see. To judge someone that you have never even met based on the actions of others is...UNJUST!"

"After spending a good deal of time in Mindar, I was appointed to be an ambassador of peace between my race and the people of Mindar. ...And so, I have done that from that very day until today."

"But you should also know that when I spoke with my family and friends, they decided to continue living in the Dark Depths. They could NOT fully bring themselves to believe that the race of man was now trustworthy. That is why you do NOT see any other sea dragons in Mindar or hear of any other sightings of my kind around the world."

The great sea dragon of ancient legend then paused for a moment before saying to them, "Now, you know my story, my friends."

Everyone was quiet...each one searching for the right words to say to their friend.

"I don't know what to say, bud...," Mark began. "But I'm really sorry about what happened to your family and to all of your friends!"

"Yeah, me, too, Z. I'm real sorry about it!" Sasper added.

"My dear friend," the Princess began. "I did not know...Madison never spoke to me of this."

"What happened took place a very long time ago. Now, I have a wonderful life with all of you!" Zarden responded. "I have friends who have seen fit to risk their own lives to help me and my family, and for that I will always be grateful to each one of you!"

"We'll find a way to help your dad get better, no matter what!" Mark said loudly.

"That's what friends do!" Sasper added.

"They are always there for each other!" Nadee said firmly.

"We've got your back, Z! You can count on us!" Madison declared.

The great sea dragon smiled.

~ The Terrifying Megatooth ~

A short time later, Nadee said to Zarden, "I've been thinking about something that you said."

"Yes, Princess?" he replied.

"You spoke of ZaMar and the other outcasts…," she began.

"What about them?" Zarden responded to her.

"Is it possible that they could have somehow survived after they left your city?"

"Yeah, what about it, Z? It's a mighty big ocean out there," Sasper added.

"It is highly unlikely that they could have survived. The undersea world is incredibly beautiful, but it can also be quite deadly, as well," Zarden reminded them.

"Well, I sure hope that you don't run out of juice down here, Maddy," Sasper said.

"NO WORRIES, fuzzy! I've got a lifetime supply!" and Madison laughed.

Nadee stared out into the darkness, "This is so completely different from our world above."

"Very soon we will begin to see some of the strange inhabitants of this world," Zarden said.

With wide eyes the curious travelers pressed their faces up against Madison's outer wall.

Then, as if right on cue, a small fish completely covered with iridescent lights from head to tail swam directly in front of the bubble-sphere.

"Hey! Check out this little guy. I think he's called a "Lanternfish," Sasper announced to everyone.

"...And that one swimming over there, I'm pretty sure he's called a "Fangtooth," and there goes a, oh, what was that name again? Oh, yeah...that's a "Stoplight Loosejaw"! WOW!! THIS IS SO COOL!" Sasper said very excitedly.

"Dude, how in the world do you know all this stuff??" Mark asked his canine friend.

"One night Michael was up pretty late and he started flippin' channels on the TV. He ran across a National Geographic special on deep sea life...the kinds of strange creatures that lived at that depth, how they survived, and so on. It was some really fascinatin' stuff, so I sat down next to him on the couch, and I started watchin' it, too."

"So, what can you tell us about these creatures, Sasper?" the Princess asked.

"Well, you see the light that's shining through them. The scientists call it..."Bioluminescence". There's a chemical reaction happening inside of their bodies, and it makes them "light" up that way!"

"...And you see that little light-thingy dangling out there in front of them?" Sasper added.

"Yeah, what about it?" Mark asked curiously.

"Well, since everything's so dark down here they use that "light" to attract their prey right to 'em. It's kinduv' the same way the fishermen back home use a shiny lure to attract the fi...uh, oh...."

"Uh, oh? Uh, oh, what, dude?" Mark said, becoming concerned.

"I just thought of somethin'...Maddy's givin' off a whole lot of light down here and if some hungry deep-sea predator was out lookin' for its next meal and they just happen to see it..."

"You're sayin' it'll come after us!?!" Mark exclaimed.

Suddenly, a long row of lights appeared somewhere off in the distance. Judging by the number of lights they could see whatever this thing was...it was...HUGE! With their hearts racing, they pressed their faces up against Madison's outer wall and looked out into the darkness that surrounded them.

Then...THEY SAW IT!!

A gigantic deep-sea creature, close to 40 feet in length, with a mouthful of razor-sharp teeth, moving very slowly and deliberately towards them. They stood there trembling with fear, but their eyes were transfixed on the terrifying beast!

"When am I gonna' learn ta' keep my big mouth shut!!" Mark muttered to himself.

About twenty feet away from them, the terrifying creature stopped moving. Then it spoke to them in a very deep voice...I AM MEGATOOTH!! ...And you, strange-looking creatures...are about to become...MY DINNER!!"

"Uh, Madison, if you've got any great ideas..." Mark whispered.

"Just one, kid...LET'S GIT' OUTTA' HERE!!" she yelled.

Madison took off like a rocket ship with the deadly undersea predator right behind her, the massive creatures' powerful jaws snapping furiously at them from just inches away.

"He's right on your tail, Maddy!" Mark screamed.

"Tell me somethin' I don't know!" Madison yelled back.

"We have to find a way to escape from Megatooth!" Nadee shouted.

Suddenly, Sasper had an idea!

"Maddy, see that mountain over there? I want ya' ta' head right for it!" he shouted at the top of his lungs.

"Dude, are you crazy!?!" Mark screamed at the little white dog.

"JUST TRUST ME, BRO'!" Sasper quickly shot back.

Then, Sasper looked back at their pursuer and yelled, "Hey! What was yur' name again...Megabutt?? Yur' way TOO SLOW, dude! My 98-year-old grandmother swims faster than you do!!"

Sasper then stuck out his little pink tongue at the pursuing deep-sea beast and followed that up by blowing several sweet little puppy-dog kisses at him.

"You dare to mock me, tiny white creature??" Megatooth screamed in rage. "I am going to enjoy eating you first!!"

"Nyah! Nyah! Nyah! Nyah! You've got stinky fish-breath, Megamouth!!" Sasper teased.

"Dude, what are you doing?!? Mark screamed at Sasper.

"It's called strategy, bro'!" Sasper said firmly.

"Strategy!?! Have you just lost your furry mind?? You're gonna' get us all killed!!" Mark screamed at him.

Meanwhile, Madison continued to race at break-neck speed towards the undersea mountain. Beneath the mountain itself there was a deep undersea chasm stretching out in both directions.

"Ready, Madison?" Sasper asked.

"Ready, Fuzzy!" she replied.

"We're about ta' go splat on the side of a big mountain! " DO SOMETHING!!" Mark shouted.

Just twenty feet away from the undersea mountain, Sasper screamed... "DOUSE THE LIGHT!!"

To Megatooth, his intended prey had somehow just completely...VANISHED!

Madison banked hard to the left and then raced away, but Megatooth with absolutely NO time at all to change directions, slammed head-first right into the side of the undersea mountain! Stunned by the tremendous impact, the fearsome deep-sea creature slowly sank into the yawning undersea chasm just below it.

"Ooooo...that's gotta' hurt...A LOT!!" Sasper said, and he grinned! "That'll teach ya' ta' mess around with *Danger Dog* and his buds!" Then, the little white dog threw back his head and howled in triumph!

"Man, that was close!" Mark said in a hushed voice.

"Well done, my friends!" Zarden shouted as he swam up to the bubble-sphere.

"That was brilliant strategy, Sasper and Madison!" the Princess said.

"I agree!" and Sasper grinned.

"Not bad, fuzzy! Not bad at all!" Madison added.

"Okay! I'm still completely in the dark here, guys."

"Can someone please explain it to me?" Mark asked.

"Think comic books, dude! The good guy razzes the bad guy to get him off of his game. He's tryin' ta' make him so angry that he gets careless and does somethin' really stupid! Then, it's GAME OVER for the bad guy!!"

"Something like slamming right into the side of a huge mountain?" Mark asked him.

"BINGO! I'd say things worked out perfectly!" Sasper said happily.

"My friends, we do not know the extent of Megatooth's injuries. So, I suggest that we leave here now!" the undersea princess advised them.

"I'm with ya' on that one, Princess," Madison replied, and she quickly jetted them away to a place of safety.

As they continued their journey to Zarden's home, Mark was still replaying in his mind everything that had happened earlier.

"So, did you guys' mind-link back there, or what?" Mark asked Madison.

"In a crazy situation like that one there's NO time to stop and talk things out!" Madison said firmly. "I sensed what Sasper was thinkin' an' I thought it might work."

"Well, I'm just happy it all worked out!" Mark shared.

"As am I, Mark!" the Princess added.

"So, it looks like Megatooth's gonna' be out of commission for a while. So, what's next Z?" Sasper asked his friend.

~ Discovering Safe Haven ~

"We must find the 3 glow-stones! Our city is hidden away from view inside of a mountain and the glow-stones serve as a "marker" to help us in finding it. Zarden revealed.

"So, what are these Glow-Stones?!?" Mark questioned.

"When we first arrived here, we discovered many large luminescent rocks just lying there in the sand all around us. We quickly realized that they could be of incredible help to us. Not only because of the brilliant light that they give off, but they also radiate heat and that would serve to help keep us warm. It's safe to say that without the discovery of the glow-stones we would NOT have survived for very long in these hostile conditions."

"We must be getting close to... THERE!" the great sea dragon shouted, and he raced ahead of them.

Some 50 feet away from where they were, 3 large stones shone brightly in the darkness.

"Come, my friends, we have successfully reached the end of our journey!" Zarden said happily.

As they stood next to the glow-stones, Zarden leaned down and touched the one in the middle with his long snout. It immediately began to vibrate, and glow even brighter than before.

"Hey! What's with that weird humming sound?" Mark asked and he looked around.

"Yeah, it sounds like a melody from some song," Sasper added.

"It is quite...BEAUTIFUL!" and Nadee gave an appreciative smile.

"I am signaling the guardians of the city that we have arrived," Zarden explained to them.

"So, yur' basically ringin' the doorbell and then waitin' for somebody to come and answer it," Sasper stated.

A few seconds later, 2 huge sea dragons appeared from somewhere out of the darkness.

"Hail! Great Zarden!" one of them said.

"We celebrate your safe return to us, noble son of Zarak," the other one said. "Now, you and your friends will follow us inside" and they quickly turned away.

Sasper whispered to Mark, "Can you believe this, dude?!? We're somewhere in the very deepest part of the ocean and about ta' enter a hidden city!"

"Yeah, how cool is that?!?" Mark whispered back.

"Okay, boys an' girls, just keep yur' hands inside of the ride at all times," Madison instructed them.

Carefully, they began to make their way along the pathway that stretched out in front of them.

"Hey, guys! Check it out! There are solid stone walls on both sides of us!" Mark exclaimed.

"I'm thinkin' that we're inside some kinduv' tunnel and it goes right through the mountain!" Sasper said excitedly. "This is so COOL! It's just like the rock city of Petra over in Israel!" he added.

"When were you in Israel, dude?" Mark said surprised.

"Ever heard of the internet, bro'?" Sasper chided him.

"Well, that explains all of the dog-hair that I keep finding on the computer keys!" and Mark laughed out loud.

"I believe that this was all strategically designed by someone," Nadee said.

"What do you mean, strategically, Nadee?" Mark asked.

"Any attacking enemy would be at a very strong disadvantage if they tried to enter the city this way. It is so narrow across that only a few of the invaders could enter it at one time," she added.

"...And that would make the city much easier to defend, right?" Mark said.

"Exactly!" the dark-haired Princess replied.

"It's pretty obvious that somebody knew what they were doin' here," Madison observed.

Before long they reached the end of the tunnel and they cautiously exited from it. As they did a huge mountain rose up directly in front of them to greet them. Cut into the side of the mountain itself there was a series of caves and in front of each one of the caves there was a glow-stone giving off light.

"It looks like some crazy all lit-up beehive!" Sasper exclaimed.

"It's sooooo...BEAUTIFUL!" the Princess said as the light danced in her pretty dark eyes.

"So, does your family live in one of those caves, Z?" Mark asked his friend.

"Yes, Mark, they do. Welcome, my friends, to the city of Safe Haven... my home!" Zarden said proudly.

The huge sea dragon's eyes then began to fill up with tears. He had been gone for so very long and now, at long last, he had finally returned home. As he stood there so many feelings swept over him.

Nadee placed her hand on Zarden's long neck and gently patted it. "Everything will be alright, my friend," she said softly to him.

From above them, a sea dragon emerged from one of the many caves and it began to move very quickly in their direction.

"Mother!" Zarden shouted, and he raced upward to meet her. As they met, they touched affectionately with their long snouts.

"I came as fast as I could. How is my father?" Zarden asked her with great concern.

"He is resting comfortably. I will take you to him." Zarden's mother said to him.

Her eyes then drifted over to Madison and the ones who were standing inside of her. "Who are these with you, Zarden?" she asked.

"These are my friends," and he smiled broadly.

"Mother, this is Madison," Zarden announced.

"Ma'am," Madison replied respectfully.

"...And may I present to you, Nadee, the Royal Princess of the city of Mindar."

Nadee bowed gracefully and respectfully in the direction of Zarden's mother.

"Welcome to our city, Nadee, Royal Princess of Mindar", and she smiled warmly at her.

"...And these are my good friends from the world that is above us, Mark and Sasper."

"It's very nice to meet you!" Mark said, and he smiled at Zarden's mother.

"I'm very happy to meet you, too, Momma Z," Sasper added.

"Welcome to you both!" Zarden's mother said to them.

"When my friends learned of father's illness, they immediately offered to help," Zarden shared.

"Their help is most welcome...and please, everyone, call me, Zania," and she smiled. "Now, please come with me." Then she turned and headed towards the cave.

Zania entered the cave, and they followed close behind her. Shortly, they reached the end of the cave, where Zarden's father was now resting.

Upon seeing his son, Zarden's father lifted up his huge head and said, "My son has returned!"

"FATHER!" Zarden shouted and he raced to his side and leaned down close to him. Their snouts touched tenderly, and they celebrated being together once more.

"When I heard of your illness I came as fast as I could, Father," Zarden said. "...And these are my good friends. They are here to help us!"

"Welcome to you all!" Zarden's father said happily. "You are quite brave to have made the journey here to the Dark Depths," he added.

"Father, what must be done for you to recover from your illness?" Zarden asked.

"He needs a medicine that can only be made from the *Red Flowers*," his mother stated.

"Where can we find these Red Flowers?" Zarden asked his mother.

"We are not certain that it even exists, but if it does, we have some idea of where to look for it," Zania said.

"Then, we will begin our search at once," Zarden said firmly.

"NO, my son!" Zarden's father's voice suddenly echoed throughout the family cave.

"But Father, there can be NO delay! We must..." Zarden began to say.

"You and your friends must be exhausted from your journey here, my Son. You must rest and take some time to regain your strength. My condition is now stable, so I am out of danger. You can begin your search for the Red Flowers in the morning."

Zarden turned to Zania, "Mother??"

"Listen to your father, Zarden. He knows how he is feeling, and a goodnight's rest will greatly help you and your friends."

Zarden stood there for a long moment...thinking. "Very well, then. I will respect your wishes on this. "We will begin our search for the Red Flowers first thing in the morning," he said.

Zania then said, "...And as for the sleeping arrangements for tonight, I suggest that Madison and the Princess can stay here with us. Zarden, you, and your friends should be quite comfortable spending the night in our family guest cave."

"As you wish, Mother," Zarden replied.

"I appreciate the thought, guys, but I DON'T sleep!" Madison stated.

"You DON'T sleep at all?!? That is MOST unusual, my new friend," Zarden's dad said.

"Yeah, I hear that a lot!" and Madison snickered.

"These guys, on the other hand, definitely need to rest up after the long trip down here," Madison shared.

"Hey! Wait a minute. I just thought of something," Mark blurted out.

"Yeah, what's that, kid?" Madison asked.

"Well, if you're staying here with them, and Sasper and I go sleep in the guest cave, then we're gonna' be on the outside of you, right?" Mark asked with some concern.

"Yeah, so?" Madison replied.

"So, we WON'T be protected by you anymore! Remember what you told us...tremendous water pressure...crack like an eggshell...did you forget about that?" Mark asked in a panicked voice.

"It WON'T happen, guys!" Madison said firmly.

"...And, why NOT?" Sasper asked.

"...Because a part of me is gonna' go with you to the guest cave so you'll still be protected from any kinduv' danger, that's why," Madison stated.

"Seriously?? You can do that!?!" Mark said surprised.

"SURE! Don't cha' remember how I divided inta' 6 bubble-spheres to get us past Z awhile back?" she reminded them.

Mark and Sasper stood there just looking at each other.

"TRUST ME! You guys WON'T be in any danger!" Madison said firmly.

"Okay! I'll prove it to you! Mark, you step outside of me first, and then Sasper, you follow him out," Madison instructed them.

Mark closed his eyes, took a deep breath, and stepped out of Madison into the cave.

As he did, a part of Madison went with him and covered him completely from head to toe.

"Hey! I'm okay out here! You were right, Madison!" Mark said, feeling very relieved.

"Now, it's yur' turn, fuzzy!" Madison prodded Sasper.

The little white dog nodded and then he phased through Madison and out into the cave.

"Well?" Madison asked.

"I'm peachy-keen!" Sasper replied happily.

"We're sorry we doubted you, Madison," Mark said.

"Yeah, we shoulda' trusted you. You've never steered us wrong before," Sasper added.

"...And I NEVER will! Don't you ever forget that!' Madison said firmly.

"Now anything changes out there you let me know about it, ASAP!" Madison advised them.

"WE WILL!" Sasper shouted.

Zarden then motioned for Mark and Sasper to climb up his back and they would go to the family guest cave for the night.

"Sleep well, everyone!" Zarden said. "We will return in the morning ready to begin our search."

"Sleep well, my friends," Nadee called out to them as they headed for the entrance to the cave.

"Alright, they're all set for tonight, so it's time for you to get some sleep, Princess," Madison said to Nadee.

"It was a long journey here. A restful sleep would be most welcome right now," the dark-haired Princess replied.

"...And that is just what you shall have," said Zarden's mother and she smiled at them.

A few moments later, Zarden, Mark, and Sasper arrived at the guest cave.

"Looks pretty dark in there, guys!" Sasper said, and he eyed the cave suspiciously.

"Suddenly, Mark and Sasper began to glow even brighter, and it completely lit up the entrance to the cave.

"Madison, are you doing this to us?" Mark asked.

"I told ya' I was comin' with ya', didn't I?" Did you guys forget already?" Madison reminded him.

"So, part of you is here with us now and part of you is back with the Princess?" Sasper questioned.

"Yeah! Pretty cool, huh?" Madison snickered.

"If you say so, Maddy, but I think it's kinduv' weird that you can do that but, hey, we can see into the cave now, so the problem is solved," Sasper said.

Shortly, they reached the very end of the cave, and they began to look around.

Sasper began to chuckle to himself.

"Somethin' funny, dude?" Mark asked.

"Check it out, bro'...we're now standin' in the "original" man cave!" and he laughed out loud.

"...Or maybe it's a dog cave?" Mark added, and he laughed, too.

"You are both completely WRONG, my friends! Anyone can plainly see that this is a...sea dragon cave!" Zarden added.

The three friends looked at each other and then they all burst out laughing at the same time.

"Listen, before we turn in for the night there is something that I want you all to see," Zarden shared.

"What's that, bud?" Mark asked his curiosity kicking in.

"Come with me,' Zarden said.

Zarden then led them to a particular section of the cave.

" I want you to see...THIS!" Zarden declared.

Everyone stared at the cave wall directly in front of them and the strange drawings that appeared on it.

"So, what are we looking at here, Z?" Mark asked.

"NO ONE in Safe Haven knows, Mark!" Zarden stated.

"Well, if ya' ask me, it looks like a buncha' drawings of some really weird-looking octopuses!" Sasper suggested.

"Octopuses, huh? Seriously, dude!?! Mark exclaimed.

"Are there any more drawings like this one on the other cave walls?" Mark asked Zarden.

"Yes!" Zarden quickly replied.

"Madison, what do you think?" Mark asked his friend.

"I think that we're just wastin' time here! We came down here to help Zarden's dad get better and that's what we should be focused on. This other stuff can wait," Madison stated.

"But aren't you even curious? I mean, we've got a real mystery on our hands here! Where did all those glow-stones come from? Who carved all those caves into the side of the mountain? ...And now there's these weird drawings on some of the cave walls! ...And, oh, by the way, we found all of this in the very deepest part of our ocean, where it's completely hidden away and no one even knows about it!" Mark stated.

"I NEVER said I wasn't interested in it. I'm sayin' helpin' Z's Dad should be our top priority and we can deal with the rest of this stuff afterwards!" Madison said firmly.

"Well, I know what I'm gonna' do tonight!" Sasper declared to everyone.

"Yeah, what's that, bud?" Mark asked him.

"I'm gonna' sleep with one eye open!" Just in case any uninvited guests decide to drop in on us!" the little white dog said very loudly.

"Yeah, me, too!" Mark quickly added.

"I will join you, my friends!" Zarden added.

"That's enough!! EVERYBODY JUST CHILL!!" Madison shouted. "NO ONE'S gonna' bother us tonight! ...And if anyone even tries to, they're gonna' live to regret it. That I can promise you!" Madison snarled.

Mark, Sasper, and Zarden just stood there quietly for a moment.

"Madison's right! All this mystery-stuff can wait!" Mark said firmly.

"I agree! We need ta' focus on helping Z's Dad now!" Sasper said.

"But now it is time for us to sleep!" Zarden declared.

In no time at all everyone had fallen fast asleep in the cave.

~ The Search for the Red Flowers ~

The next day began, and everyone was eager to begin the search for the Red Flowers that would help Zarden's father to recover from his illness.

"Alright, rise an' shine, guys! Time for us ta' go find those healin' flowers," Madison said.

The group of adventurers quickly made their way back to the family cave.

As they re-entered it, Zarden's mom was there to greet them.

"Did everyone sleep well?" she asked them.

"I slept just like a lil' baby, Momma Z," Sasper replied.

"I knew that you would, Sasper," Zania said.

Zarden's father then addressed the group, "While you are out searching for the Red Flowers you must be ready at all times to defend yourself. Megatooth is just one of the many dangers that we face down here."

"We'll be okay out there! You just keep fightin' this thing an' we'll be back just as quick as we can with yur' medicine!" Madison said firmly.

"Come, my friends!" Zarden shouted.

They soon found themselves once more in the unnerving blackness of the Dark Depths.

"You know, something could be out there just waitin' ta' make a snack out of us, dude!" Sasper said, and he pressed his furry face up against Madison's outer wall.

"You scared, bro'?" Mark asked Sasper.

"ME!?! NO WAY! *Danger Dog* is NEVER scared! I live for moments like this and…"

"Do you see anything?" Nadee whispered from somewhere behind them.

"YEEAAAAAA!!" Mark and Sasper screamed in unison and they both jumped about 2 feet!! "NADEE!! PLEASE…DON'T DO THAT!!" Mark shouted scolding her.

"You scared some of the fur right off of me!" Sasper complained.

"I'M SORRY!" the undersea princess replied.

"Hey! Stop with all that bouncin' around! You'll give me an upset stomach!" Madison growled.

"Madison, you don't even have a stomach! At least, I don't think you have one," Mark said.

"That's totally besides the point!" Madison snapped.

Zarden swam up to the bubble-sphere and pointed somewhere off to their right.

"This is where we will begin our search," he announced.

"Alright, everyone just git' out there and start lookin' for these Red Flowers thingy!" Madison urged.

Nadee, Mark, and Sasper then phased out of Madison and into the water. The bright glow that Madison was giving off helped them to see much better in the darkness.

"Alright, guys…let's find the Red Flowers and get it back to Z's dad pronto," Madison said loudly.

"...And if there's any kinduv' trouble, I'll bring all of you right back here inside of me in less than a nano-second. Then, we'll get out of here really FAST!" Madison said.

After about twenty minutes of searching unsuccessfully for the Red Flowers, fear and worry began to slowly creep into their minds.

"This is like lookin' for a needle in a haystack, bud," Sasper whispered to Mark.

"I know that, but we just can't give up. Zarden's dad is counting on us," Mark replied.

Sensing the anxiety that was building up in his friends, Zarden addressed the group saying, "My friends, I know our task may seem impossible, but we all must have faith that we will succeed!"

Suddenly, Madison screamed..."EVERYONE!! BACK INSIDE!!"

"What's wrong, Madison??" Mark immediately questioned.

Everyone peered out intently into the darkness from the safety of the bubble-sphere.

"Is it Megatooth again?" Nadee asked.

"NO! It's NOT Megatooth! But there's somethin' out there, and it's definitely headed in our direction!" Madison responded.

"Whatever this new threat is we must deal with it very quickly so there will still be time enough left to save my father!" Zarden shouted.

Then, from somewhere out of the darkness, a voice was heard...

"You shouldn't be worrying about your father, Zarden. You should be worrying about what's going to happen next to you and your friends!"

"That...voice! It...it can't be..." Zarden said in a hushed town.

Suddenly, a group of sea dragons emerged from somewhere out of the darkness.

"Greetings, my one-time, brother," the one in the front shouted at the bubble-sphere.

"ZaMar!?! You're...ALIVE!?! I thought you were long dead!" Zarden stammered.

"I'm SORRY to disappoint you, but as you can now plainly see, I am still very much alive."

"You and your friends on the other hand WON'T be for very much longer!" ZaMar shouted. "At long last I will have my revenge on you and your family!!"

"What happened to us was a long time ago, ZaMar. Everyone lost something of great value to them on that tragic day," Zarden shouted.

"Did you lose your loving parents as I did, Zarden? NO! YOU DID NOT!" ZaMar screamed at Zarden.

"Your father's extremely naive idea that there could be peace between our race and the race of man cost both my mother and father their lives!" he stated.

"...And, for that I am truly sorry, ZaMar!" Zarden said softly and he bowed his head.

"Your sorry will NOT bring them back to me!" ZaMar screamed at him.

"But I do know why you have returned here, and you won't succeed in your mission!" ZaMar added.

"What do you mean, ZaMar?" Zarden questioned his former friend.

"Word gets around down here very quickly, my old friend. When I heard of your father's grave illness, I knew that you would immediately return to Safe Haven to try and save him. So, all I really had to do was just bide my time and wait for you to show up," ZaMar said.

"But I should also tell you that while my friends and I were waiting for you to arrive here, we removed all of the Red Flowers that were growing here. So, now there is NONE left for you and your friends to find. ...And that means that your father will surely DIE! Unless..."

"...Unless what, ZaMar? Out with it!" Zarden demanded to know.

"You fight me in a...Death-Match! If you somehow defeat me, I will give you your precious Red Flowers and you father will LIVE to see another day!"

"I DO NOT wish to kill you, ZaMar! Once, we were brothers," Zarden said.

"That was long ago, Zarden. We are brothers NO MORE!! ...And I DO wish to kill you! I wish it very much!!" and ZaMar smiled wickedly.

"Those are my terms! Do you accept them? Yes, or no?" ZaMar snarled at him.

"If it is the only way I can save my father, then, so be it!" Zarden declared.

"There is one other little thing that you all should know before the contest begins," ZaMar warned.

"I am listening..." Zarden answered.

"Once I have killed you, your friends will die next!" and ZaMar laughed.

"WHY?! They have NOTHING to do with this, ZaMar! This is just between you and I," Zarden challenged him.

"They stand with you, and they will fall with you, as well!" ZaMar screamed.

"Then, grant me a final moment with them before we begin our contest," Zarden requested.

"So granted," ZaMar quickly replied.

Zarden then turned away and quickly headed in the direction of the bubble-sphere.

"My friends, I wish it had not come to this," Zarden said softly.

"You can take him, bud! I know you can!" Mark said.

"Just defeating him will NOT be enough, my young friend! I must also KILL him!" Zarden stated.

"Zarden, it was our decision to come here with you. We did not know what the future held for any of us. We only knew that our friend needed us. We have lived together, and, if necessary, we will die together, as well!" the undersea princess said with strong conviction in her voice.

The great sea dragon nodded!

"NO ONE in this world could ever have greater friends than all of you! I love each one of you very much!" Zarden shared.

Then, he turned to face ZaMar in the undersea Death Match.

"I will do what I must!" he shouted.

"Can't we do something to help him, Madison?" Mark asked.

"NO!" Madison answered him firmly.

"Why not?" Sasper questioned.

"This fight of theirs is all about *honor*. We have ta' completely stay out of it an' just hope that Z can somehow find a way ta' come out on top!" Madison stated.

Everyone watched intently as Zarden and ZaMar began to circle each other.

"How long have I dreamed of this moment...of feeling my jaws wrapped tightly around your neck...of hearing you beg me for your life before I finally put an end to it!" ZaMar threatened.

"Your victory will NOT come easily, ZaMar, for we are very evenly matched," Zarden replied.

The two combatants continued to circle each other looking for just the right opportunity to strike. The tension grew with each minute that went by. ...And then, there was a tremendous flurry of twisting bodies and snapping jaws!

It was...OVER!

Zarden's powerful jaws were now tightly wrapped around ZaMar's neck. One violent bite and Zarden would be the clear victor of the Death-Match.

"KILL...ME...NOW...AND...END...MY...PAIN!!" ZaMar whispered to Zarden.

Zarden looked over at his friends, his eyes searching theirs...and asking the question...*What should I do?* If he failed to kill ZaMar then he and his friends would immediately be put to death! If he killed ZaMar could he live with the terrible knowledge of what he had done? Zarden closed his eyes for a long moment...and then...his jaws loosened their grip on ZaMar's neck.

"I will NOT do this evil thing! I love you as a brother, ZaMar!" Zarden shouted.

"Then, you are a FOOL!" ZaMar snarled at him.

"Perhaps, but I still believe that the ZaMar I once knew still exists somewhere inside of you. Hate has poisoned your life-spirit for so very long but now it is time for you to finally be free of it!"

There was a long moment of silence as everyone looked on anxiously. What would happen next?

Finally, ZaMar shouted ..."Bring him the medicine!"

"Thank you, ZaMar!" Zarden said.

One of the sea dragons with ZaMar turned and left, but he quickly returned with several Red Flowers.

"With this your father will live," ZaMar said.

"...And what of you and your friends, ZaMar? What will you do now?" Zarden asked him.

"I...DO NOT know. For so very long my tremendous hatred of you gave me a purpose! I lived each day in the hope that I would have an opportunity to gain my revenge."

"...And how do you feel now, ZaMar?" Zarden asked him.

"I feel...empty...and uncertain," ZaMar replied softly.

"Then return with us to Safe Haven!" Zarden challenged him.

"Return to Safe Haven!?! We CANNOT! We are outcasts! We would be SHUNNED!!"

"Return with me now and I will stand with you before the Great Council and request that you and your fellow outcasts be welcomed back to Safe Haven."

"You would do that? After I just tried so very hard to kill you?" ZaMar asked.

"I would do it for the brother whom I had lost and have now found again," Zarden said firmly.

"Let me discuss it with the others," and ZaMar turned and headed over to them.

Several minutes later the leader of the outcasts returned and said, "We will return with you."

Zarden smiled and said, "It is time for a new beginning, my friend!"

~ A New Beginning ~

Upon returning to Safe Haven, they quickly headed for the cave of Zarden's family.

It had been decided enroute that this should be a private moment for just the family members, so Zarden entered the cave alone.

As Zarden reached the cave's end, he was shocked to see that not only was his father out of bed, but that he was also moving around the cave quite easily.

"Father, I DO NOT understand...you are recovered?? How can this be!?!" Zarden said, completely shocked by what he was now seeing.

"Your father has fully recovered from his illness," Zania shared happily.

"Fully recovered?!? Please mother, explain..." Zarden asked her.

"It turns out that what your father really needed was to see...YOU!" his mother revealed.

"To see me??" Zarden replied.

"The love that parents have for their children is something incredibly...POWERFUL!! Your father has been missing you terribly lately. So much so that he became heartsick. He wanted to spend some time with you...his precious son!" and Zania smiled.

Zarden turned towards his father, "Father, I am so happy that you are well now!"

"Did Megatooth give you any trouble during your search?" his father asked.

"NO! Megatooth never appeared to trouble us, but something completely unexpected did happen," Zarden shared with his father.

Meanwhile, on the outside of the cave everyone was getting better acquainted with each other.

"So, tell me, how do land-walkers such as yourselves get involved in a great adventure under the sea?" ZaMar asked.

"It is quite a remarkable story, ZaMar!" Nadee replied.

"You guys ever heard of a wizard by the name of Ka-Lan?" Mark asked ZaMar.

"...Only in very frightened whispers," the sea dragon replied.

"Well, we threw down with the biggest, baddest, evilest wizard on the whole planet, and we came out on top!" Sasper said proudly.

"You defeated the wizard Ka-Lan!?!" ZaMar exclaimed with great surprise.

"Well, it took all of us working together, but yeah... we fulfilled an ancient prophecy and saved both the undersea and the surface worlds from total destruction at the hands, er, hand, of the wizard," Sasper said excitedly.

"We would hear much more about this Great Battle," ZaMar said, and everyone moved in closer to each other.

Meanwhile, back inside the cave, Zarden finished telling his father about what had happened to them while they were out searching for the Red Flowers.

"ZaMar and the others...STILL ALIVE!?!" Zarak exclaimed. "It is a miracle that they somehow survived entirely on their own for all these years!" he observed.

"Father, they have returned here to Safe Haven with us. They wish to become a part of us once more. I told ZaMar that I would petition the Great Council on their behalf."

"That will NOT be necessary, my son," his father said.

"But I MUST, Father! I have given them my word, and so, I must keep it, "Zarden explained.

"I said that it was unnecessary because the Great Council decided long ago that if they should ever one day return to us, they would immediately be welcomed back to Safe Haven."

"Father, I...THANK YOU! They will be overjoyed to hear this," and Zarden smiled happily.

"Then, go and tell them, my son...and bring ZaMar here to me. I wish to speak to him alone."

"As you wish, Father. I will return very shortly with ZaMar," and he turned and headed for the cave's entrance.

As Zarden exited from the cave, everyone immediately stopped their conversations.

The great sea dragon roared, "MY FATHER WILL LIVE!!"

A loud cheer went up!

Zarden looked over at ZaMar and said, "ZaMar, my father wishes to speak to you."

ZaMar looked back at the other outcasts and then went with Zarden into the cave.

As they entered the main room, Zarak shouted happily, "WELCOME to our home, ZaMar!! I am so thankful that you and your friends have returned safely to us!"

"Hail! Great Zarak! ...And I celebrate with you that you have recovered from your illness!"

"ZaMar, you should know that you and your friends are welcome to return to our community!" and he smiled at him.

"That is indeed wonderful news! But, if I may, I would like to ask you one question," ZaMar said.

"Then ask, ZaMar, and I will answer you," Zarak replied.

"Why is it that no one ever came and searched for us?"

"The idea was proposed from time to time, but we had no way of knowing if you were alive or dead...or where you might be in the great vastness of the sea. The Great Council decided that it was just too dangerous to send out a search party," Zarak revealed.

"I... understand," ZaMar said softly.

"But you have miraculously returned to us, ZaMar, and I think we should focus on that," Zarak suggested.

"Yes, Noble Zarak, it is time to leave the past behind," ZaMar said.

"But it is important that you understand how much we truly loved your mother and father. For so long I carried within me the guilt of what happened to them on that tragic day," Zarak said softly. "We are truly sorry, ZaMar, and we can only hope that someday you can forgive us."

ZaMar stood there quietly. "I know how much my parents loved you and Zania," he said. "I believe that they would want me to forgive you, and so Great Zarak...I CHOOSE THIS DAY TO FORGIVE YOU!"

With tears in his eyes Zarak said to the young sea dragon, "Thank you, ZaMar! Your mother and father would be very proud of you."

"Tonight, we will hold a wonderful celebration to welcome you and your friends back to our community," Zarak shouted.

"Till tonight then," ZaMar replied.

Zarak then turned to Zania, "My wife, I have a wonderful idea, but we must act very quickly."

As Zarden and ZaMar exited the cave, Madison shouted, "So, what's the verdict?"

"We are outcasts...NO MORE!!" ZaMar shouted happily to everyone.

A huge cheer went up!

"...And tonight, there will be a great celebration to welcome all of you back to Safe Haven!" Zarden roared.

Another loud cheer went up!

~ Joyous Celebration ~

That night was a joyous one indeed and everyone in Safe Haven turned out for it.

There was plenty of singing and dancing, and smiles were everywhere to be seen.

Zarden's father served as the Master of Ceremonies for the festivities, and he spoke to the large assembly saying, "My friends, tonight is a very special night! Be sure to take a moment and welcome all of those who were once called *outcasts* back to Safe Haven. Please, make sure they know how happy we are that they have returned safely to us!"

A huge cheer came from the crowd.

Later that night, Zarak glanced over at Zania and said to her, "I think it is time, my wife."

Zania nodded at her husband.

"Time for what, Father?" Zarden asked.

"You will see, my son," Zarak replied.

"ZaMar?" Zarak called out. We would like to speak to you for a moment if we may."

"Of course, Great Zarak," Zamar answered, and he quickly moved towards them.

Everyone looked out at the joy-filled scene that was taking place in Safe Haven on this night.

"Your friends seem quite happy to be back, ZaMar," Zarak said.

"THEY ARE! Our time away from Safe Haven was NOT an easy one," ZaMar shared.

"My wife and I have something for you and your friends to consider," Zarak said.

"...And what is that, Great Zarak?" ZaMar asked.

"In order to help all of you feel at home that much quicker the Great Council has approved of, well, let's call it...an adoption process. Several of our families have come forward willing to accept each one of your friends as a part of their own family!"

"They will be so happy to have a family of their very own once more," ZaMar said.

"...And ZaMar, Zania and I...we want you to become a part of our family, as well," Zarak said.

"A part of...your family?!? ZaMar said softly, tears forming in the corners of his eyes.

"Yes, ZaMar. We know that we can never replace your wonderful mother and father, but we can promise to always be there for you...from this moment and going forward!" and Zania smiled warmly at ZaMar.

"To be a part of a loving family again is more than I ever dreamed possible," ZaMar said softly.

"Then say *yes*, my brother!" Zarden roared.

"YES!" ZaMar shouted at the top of his lungs.

"Then, it is settled!" Zarak said firmly.

"Welcome to our family, ZaMar!" Zania said, and she nudged him gently with her snout.

"Now, go and tell your friends the great news!" Zarak shouted.

"I WILL! THANK YOU!" ZaMar said firmly.

Then, ZaMar looked at Zarden and said, "Come, my brother," and the two sea dragons disappeared into the huge crowd.

Mark looked down and saw that Sasper was sobbing uncontrollably.

"Why are you crying, bro'?" Mark asked his friend.

"Just can't help it! This reminds me of the night that you and your family came to the shelter and picked me to go home with you! I was so HAPPY! After waiting for so long, I finally had a home of my very own," Sasper shared.

"...And you always will, bro'...forever and ever!" and Mark placed his hand gently on Sasper's shoulder.

It was a very special moment for the two of them.

The night eventually wore down and it was time for everyone to finally get some sleep.

Mark and Sasper soon found themselves back in the guest cave and preparing to bed down.

"What a NIGHT!" Mark said happily.

"You said it, man!" Sasper replied.

"Never thought I'd see a Conga line made up of sea dragons!" and Mark laughed.

"Well, we learned one thing tonight...sea dragons seriously know how to party!" and the little white dog laughed out loud.

"Hey! Speakin' of sea dragons...where's Z?" Mark asked.

"He told me he was gonna' hang out with his family," Sasper replied.

"Can't say I blame him. He seems really happy to be back home," Mark observed.

"So, changin' up subjects here…when are you and Nadee gonna' have yur' little *talk*?" Sasper asked.

"I keep looking for the right moment to do it, but everything's been so crazy since we got down here with one thing happening right after another," Mark said.

"Look! I know you're scared, bro'…I'd be scared, too," Sasper shared.

"You…scared!?" I thought *Danger Dog* NEVER got scared?" Mark teased his best friend.

"This is different. What she tells you could change the whole rest of your life, dude."

"Yeah, I know…" Mark said softly.

"But it's just gotta' be DONE! You have ta' know where you stand with her," Sasper said firmly.

"Great advice, bro!'" Mark replied.

"Okay, that'll be a nickel. C'MON, PAY UP!" and Sasper held out his little white paw to Mark.

"Why a nickel?" Mark asked curiously.

"Isn't that what Lucy always charges Charlie Brown for her great advice?" and he winked at him.

"I think you're right and it's definitely worth every penny!" and Mark smiled.

"Hey! No matter what happens with the Princess, you've always got me, dude!" Sasper said firmly.

"Thanks! I'll keep that in mind!" and Mark laughed.

"Well, we better get some sleep, so we'll be ready for the trip back home tomorrow," Mark said to Sasper.

"Yeah, time for us to go back home. Goodnight, bro'" Sasper said, and he closed his eyes.

"Goodnight, Sasper!" Mark replied.

~ Returning Home ~

The next day it was time for goodbyes to be said and the long journey home to begin.

They quickly gathered in the cave along with Zarden's family but there was one final thing that Mark wanted to do that involved the Princess.

"Nadee, before we head back home there's something I think you should see," Mark said to her.

"What is it?" Nadee replied curiously.

"I promise it won't take long," Mark added.

Then he turned to Zarden and said, "Hey, bud. Can we get a quick ride back to the guest cave?"

"Of course, my friends" Zarden replied.

A few moments later, Mark and Nadee were standing in front of the cave wall with the strange markings on it. Zarden chose to wait for them outside of the cave.

The Princess stared intently at the cave wall.

"So, what do you think, Nadee? I thought you should see this before we headed back home," Mark said to her.

"Thank you for showing this to me, Mark. So, no one here knows how the markings on the cave walls came to be?" she asked.

"No one in Safe Haven knows anything! It's a big mystery! Madison didn't know what to make of it either," Mark added.

"After we return home, I will meet with the city elders and bring this to their attention," she said.

Mark stood there for a moment...thinking. He was finally alone with the Princess. Maybe this was the right time for them to have their talk.

"Hey, there is something else I really wanted to talk to you about," Mark began.

"Yes, Mark?" the Princess replied.

But before Mark could say another word, Zarden's deep voice echoed throughout the cave.

"My friends, I think it is time that we rejoin the others," he said.

"Mark, we can talk once we are safely back in Mindar," the Princess said.

"Okay!" Mark said softly and then they exited the cave.

Very shortly, everyone had gathered next to the three glow-stones that mark the entrance to the city of Safe Haven.

"Nadee, Royal Princess of Mindar...Zania and I want to thank you for everything that you and your friends did for us...and to also thank you for always taking very good care of our son, " Zarak said.

"We were happy to help you, sir, and glad to see you are well once more. As for your son...Zarden is a part of our family!" Nadee said and she smiled affectionately.

"You are always welcome to visit with us," Zania said, and she smiled at them.

"Thanks for all your hospitality, Mr. and Mrs. Z!" Madison stated.

"We enjoyed having all of you here," Zania replied.

"Take care!" Mark said.

"I really hope we get to see you guys again someday," Sasper added.

"Well, I guess it's time for us to be headin' back," Madison said.

Madison then turned to Zarden and said, "So, ya' ready to get goin', Z?"

"I will NOT be returning with you, my friends," Zarden announced.

"Wh-a-at?!?! Why not, big guy?" Mark asked, very surprised.

"I discussed it with my family last night and they want me stay here with them awhile longer. It's what I want, too. After being apart for so very long we have a lot to catch up on. But ZaMar and I will serve as your escort at the beginning of the trip to make sure that Megatooth does not cause you any more trouble."

"We will miss you terribly, my friend, but we completely understand," Nadee said.

"Make every moment down here count, Z!" Sasper said to his friend.

"I am quite sure I will return to Mindar someday, but for now, this is where I want to be," Zarden stated. "But you should know that all of you will never be far from my heart."

"...And ours, too, bud," Mark replied.

"Well, when yur' ready to come back just let us know and we'll make all the arrangements," Madison said.

"We wish you a safe trip back home and be wary of Megatooth along the way," Zarak advised them.

"Megatooth is old and slow, Noble Zarak! We should be able to easily distract him and give our friends the opportunity to get past him safely," ZaMar said firmly.

"DO NOT be over-confident, ZaMar! Old also means they have gained a great deal of knowledge over the years. DO NOT underestimate him!" Zarak said firmly.

"Yes, Father, I will heed your sound advice," ZaMar replied, and he smiled at Zarak.

"We'll be careful, Father, I promise," Zarden added.

As Madison began to move away, Zarden and ZaMar took positions to the left and to the right to protect her.

"Just like old times, eh, ZaMar?" Zarden called out.

"I was thinking the very same thing, my brother," ZaMar responded."

They had travelled a good distance from Safe Haven when Madison suddenly shouted, "Uh, oh! Looks like we've got company!"

...And then, from out of the pitch darkness, Megatooth... APPEARED!

"This time you will NOT escape me!!" the gigantic sea-creature screamed at them.

As Megatooth came towards them, Zarden and ZaMar intercepted him.

With dazzling speed and precision timing, they swam in circles around the creature's massive head!

106

"It's working! They're distracting him!" Mark shouted.

"Now's our chance! Let's get outta' here, Maddy!" Sasper screamed at the top of his lungs.

"Be well, my friends! We will see each other again someday, I promise you!" Zarden shouted.

"Take care, bud!" Mark shouted.

"Be well, my friend!" Nadee added.

Mark, Sasper, and Nadee waved goodbye to their sea dragon friend as Madison zoomed away.

As Madison made her way ever upward the surrounding water conditions began to change.

"Hey! Check it out! Things are starting to get lighter," Mark observed.

"It means that we are nearing our home, my friends," Nadee said, and she smiled.

"Cool beans!! Next stop...Mindar!!" Sasper shouted happily.

In the far distance four familiar shapes appeared!

"Hey! Is that...?" and Mark pressed his face up against Madison's outer wall.

"It is! It's Arthur and his friends!" Nadee shouted happily.

The four huge great white sharks quickly formed a very tight circle around the bubble-sphere.

"Welcome home, everyone! It's great to see all of you!" Arthur, the Great White Shark called out.

"But where is my good friend Zarden? I do not see him with you," Arthur said concerned.

"He decided to spend some more time with his family," Mark replied.

"But he did say that he'd be comin' back to Mindar somewhere down the road," Sasper added.

"I am not really surprised by his decision. I know that he is very happy to be in Mindar, but I also know that there are times when he really misses his family," Arthur shared.

"Now, it is time to get all of you safely back to Mindar," Arthur stated.

Upon arriving at the Silver Dome, it was time to say goodbye to Arthur and his friends.

"Thanks for the escort home, guys!" Mark shouted.

"You guys are...AWESOME!!" Sasper added.

"You are quite welcome, my friends, and don't forget you are always welcome to come an' visit us sometime down at the Great Barrier Reef," Arthur said.

"Thank you for your help, Arthur," the Princess said.

"I am always happy to help you in any way that I can, Royal Princess of Mindar," Arthur said firmly.

"When things get back to normal around here, I'll come pay you a visit Artie," Madison shouted.

"I'll look forward to it, my friend!" Arthur shouted.

Then with a swish of their four powerful tails the great white sharks disappeared back into the ocean depths.

Madison and her weary passengers then phased through the Silver Dome.

Their friend, Geren, was there to greet them, as always. "Welcome home, everyone!" he said.

"We're glad to be home, Geren!" Mark said happily.

As they approached the city, trumpets began to blare announcing their arrival. The huge gathering of Mindarians and sea-dwellers cheered wildly as Madison gently touched down on the beautiful seashells of Main Street.

"WELCOME HOME, EVERYONE!" Talena shouted.

As everyone phased out of Madison, Talena raced forward and threw her arms around Nadee.

"Welcome home, my sister!" she said happily.

"But where is our good friend Zarden?" Bundar asked with a concerned look on his face.

"Zarden's fine, Bundar. He just decided to get in some more family-time," Mark explained.

"I understand. Family always matters!" Bundar said firmly.

Madison, Nadee, Mark and Sasper then began to make their way through the joyous crowd and towards the castle. Very shortly, they were standing once more in the Princess' room.

"I'm gonna' take a real quick cruise around the city and make sure everything's okay," Madison stated.

"Very good, Madison," the Princess responded.

Mark and Sasper looked on as Nadee was being updated by Lt. Tallus on what had transpired in Mindar while she was gone.

As he was finishing up his report, Sasper gave a quick tug on Mark's pants leg.

"Dude, now's your chance to finally talk to her!" he prodded Mark.

Mark watched as Lt. Tallus exited the room. He swallowed hard and then he walked with hesitant steps across the marble floor towards the beautiful undersea princess.

"Nadee?" he said softly.

"Yes, Mark?" she replied.

"I think it's time that we talked about...things...about how we really feel about each other and..." Mark NEVER finished his sentence!

The beautiful dark-haired girl threw her arms around him and kissed him! After about a minute, they finally stopped.

Then, the Royal Princess of Mindar looked up into Mark's blue-green eyes and asked him rather coyly, "So, what did you want to talk to me about, Mark Tanner?"

"I, uh, oh, never-mind," and he just stood there with a big silly grin on his face.

"I will call you later tonight, Mark," Nadee said, and then she turned and quickly walked away.

"Sounds good!" Mark replied.

Mark just stood there for a moment, then turned and walked back to Sasper who had a huge grin on his furry little face.

"Well, I guess you finally got your answer, bud. Friends DON'T lock-lips like that...EVER!" Sasper stated.

Mark smiled down at his friend and said, "No, they definitely don't!"

The sound of Madison's commanding voice interrupted the moment.

"If you two are thru messin' around here it's time ta' git you back home!" Madison said firmly.

"C'mon, Maddy, can't you see that they're in love?" Sasper teased.

"I can see it just fine, furball!" Madison snapped. "But now, it's time fur' me ta' take you guys back to the surface," she said.

Mark and Sasper phased into Madison and then she made her way towards the outer edge of the city. Then, they phased through the Silver Dome and began to head for the surface.

Madison said, "There's somethin' I need ta' tell ya, kid."

"What is it, Maddy?" Mark asked curiously.

"So, it's like this...I went to the Council on yur' behalf ta' see if they would give you visitation rights to the city."

"You did that for me!?! THANK YOU, Maddy! That would be...TOTALLY AWESOME!" Mark said excitedly.

"So, what did they say?" Mark asked hopefully.

"Well, the Council doesn't actually decide these things...it's completely left up to the people of Mindar."

"If everyone approves then you'll be able to visit anytime that you want to," Madison stated.

"Everyone!?! You mean the whole city!?!" Sasper asked.

111

"YUP! Everyone has to be okay with this, or the answer is no. If just one person in the city doesn't like the idea, then you won't be allowed in. Remember, it's their personal safety that we're talkin' about here."

"I understand. So, when will you know the results of the vote?" Mark asked Madison.

"I should know any minute now," Madison replied.

"I think ya' got a good shot at this, bro'. I really do!" Sasper said, trying to be encouraging.

"Does Nadee know anything about this?" Mark asked Madison.

"No! I didn't say anything to her cuz' I didn't want her to be disappointed," Madison answered.

"Hold on a sec…the Council's callin' me now. Uh, huh…uh, huh. Okay! I'll tell 'em."

"Well, what did they say?" Mark asked with a hopeful voice.

"Yur' in, kid!" Madison said loudly.

"YESSSSSS!" Mark shouted and he jumped for joy.

"Hey! TAKE IT EASY!" Madison shouted.

Sasper high-fived Mark and said, "I told ya', bro'! Everybody in Mindar loves you!"

"Hey! Wait a sec…what about me? Does this mean that I can visit anytime, too?" Sasper asked.

"Yur' in, too, fuzzy!" Madison replied.

"This is so COOL! Thank you, Madison, for doing this for me…for us," Mark said happily.

"I stuck my neck out for ya' on this one, kid. DON'T ever make me regret it!" Madison growled.

"I WON'T! I PROMISE YOU!" Mark said firmly.

"...An' ya' better treat Nadee really good! Remember...I know where you sleep!" Madison warned.

In the very next moment, Madison broke the surface of the water.

As the bubble sphere bobbed up and down on the incoming waves, Mark picked up Sasper and held him tightly to his chest. Then they phased out of the bubble-sphere and into the shallow water.

"Alright, guys! This is where we're gonna' part company for now," Madison said to them.

"Thanks again, Maddy...for EVERYTHING!" Mark said happily.

"Yur' welcome!" Madison replied.

Sasper let out a few excited yips of his own.

Mark and Sasper stood there on the sand as they watched Madison dip below the rolling ocean waves for a final time. Then, blue energy appeared all around them, and it quickly covered them from head-to-toe.

In the blink of an eye, they once again found themselves standing in Mark's bedroom. Only they weren't ALONE in the room!

"DUDE!! WHAT THE...!?! Michael shouted and he fell backwards onto Mark's bed.

"Uh, oh! We're BUSTED, dude!" Mark said to Sasper.

"Alright! I want answers and I want 'em…NOW!!" Michael screamed at Mark and Sasper.

Mark and Sasper just stood there looking at each other.

~

Original Artwork
for
The Blue Pearl Series

Created by:

Mr. Bill Golliher

One of the legendary artists of
"Archie Comics"